The BASILISK Princess

the lasina chronicles   book one

By Rozie Marshall

Enchanted Embers Press
PO BOX 585
Castle Rock, Colorado 80104

ISBN: 979-8-9857077-1-7 (Paperback)
ISBN: 979-8-9857077-2-4 (Hardcover)
ISBN: 979-8-9857077-0-0 (eBook)

Library of Congress Control Number: 2022901931

Any references to historical events, real people, or real places are used fictitiously. Names, characters, and places are products of the author's imagination.

Front cover image by Pixie Covers
Book design by Enchanted Embers Press
Printed by IngramSpark, in the United States of America.
Edited by Max Williams with BBB Publishing

First Enchanted Embers Press printing edition 2021.
www.roziemarshall.com

Contents

VI

Dedication

To all the women who love sex, sin, and just a touch of scales.

Mindy G and Krystal; I hope all your fantasies come true with this series. Please stop sending me pictures of your snakes, they scare the shit out of me.

To my husband; Thanks for indulging my curiosity on reptile mating habits and maybe twisting them for the purposes of this series.

To Everly Taylor, thank you for all the invaluable information on reptiles.

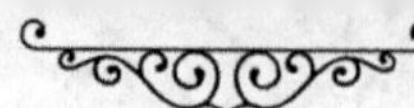

VIII

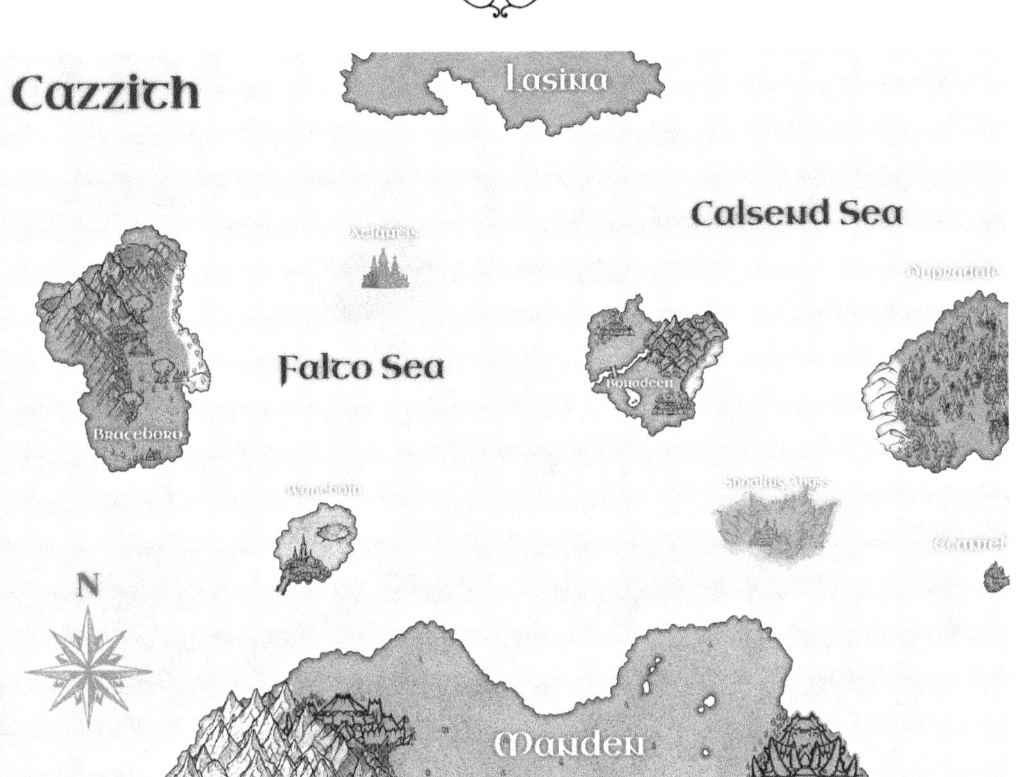

Cazzich
Lasina
Calsend Sea
Falto Sea
Braceboro
Bonadeen
Manden
N

X

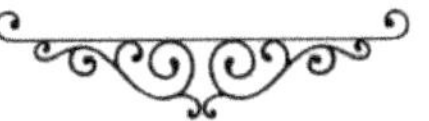

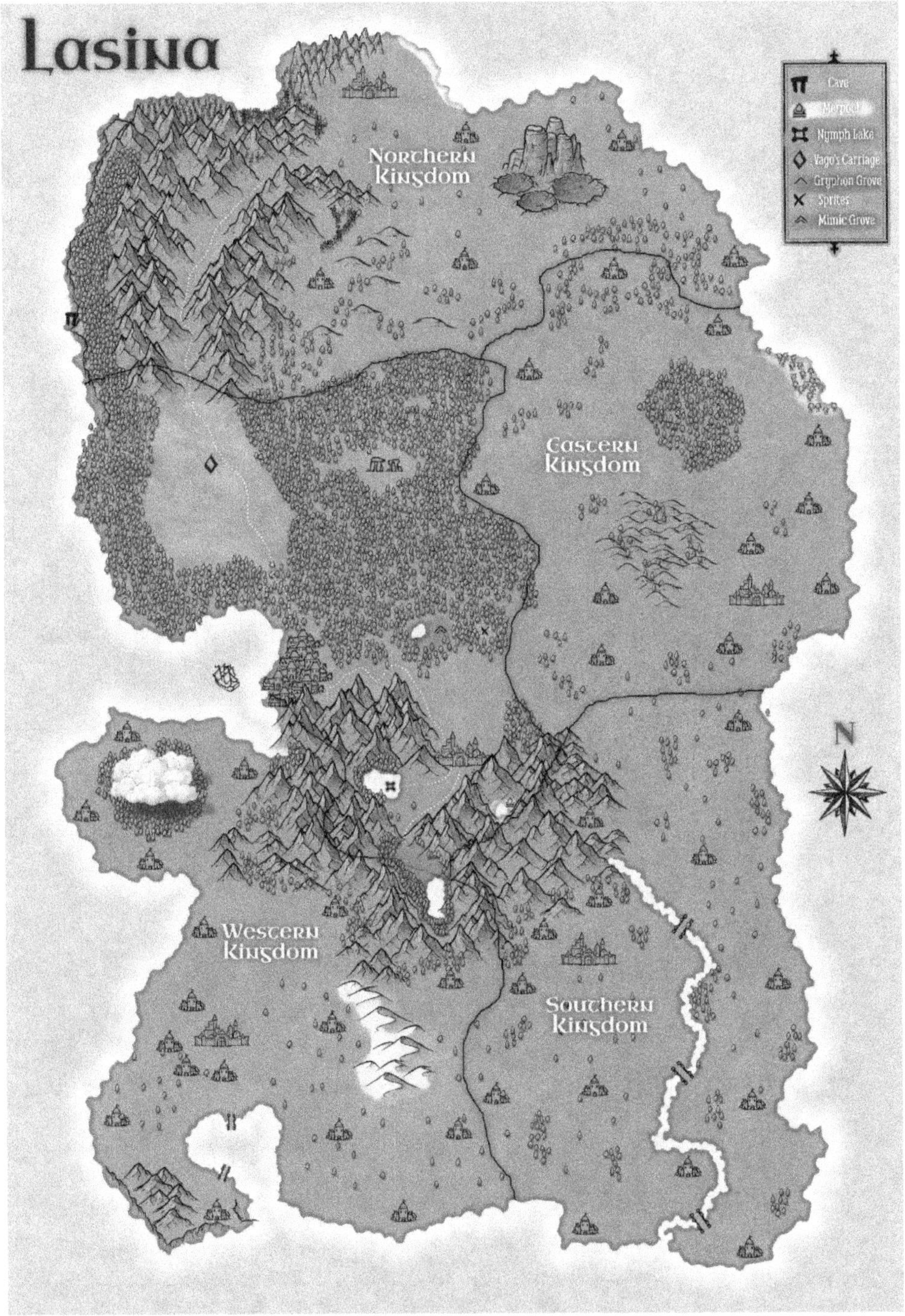
Lasina
Cave
Merpool
Nymph Lake
Vago's Carriage
Gryphon Grove
Sprites
Mimic Grove
Northern Kingdom
Eastern Kingdom
Western Kingdom
Southern Kingdom
N

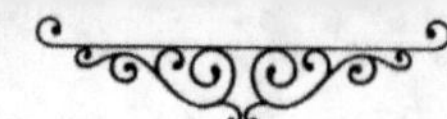

XII

"Once upon a time, there was an evil King. This King was the ruler of the North Kingdom in Lasina. The three other Kingdoms had always been at peace with the North Kingdom, until one day, the evil King killed his Queen, who was from the South Kingdom."

"But Mommy, you're not dead. How can you be dead if you're telling me this story?" a childlike voice sounded in the room.

"Maisie, if you interrupt, I won't finish your bedtime story." Clara chided once again.

"Yes, Mommy... but how did he start a war if you're alive." She continued to ask.

"Well, when the King found out his wife was about to have a child, he tried to kill her. So, she faked her death and ran away to the Earthly realm. The other Kingdoms began a war upon her disappearance, helped, of course, by the rumors of the King's beastly temper." Clara paused and shuddered as she remembered her husbands' nasty fits of rage and abuse. "The war raged for several years, until very recently when three Princes were

promised to the good Queen's daughter." Clara booped Maisie on the nose to indicate it's her, causing Maisie to giggle.

"The war ended in a very fragile peace, until the day the Princes can claim their Princess. On that day all of Lasina will be ruled by one family, ending the separation of the races that has lasted since the beginning of time." Clara smiled at Maisie the way a mother does when she knows more than she's telling.

"Mommy, can you tell me about the monsters again?" Maisie's voice was filled with excited curiosity. "And tell me about the Princes."

"Well now... Miss Maisie, the three handsome Princes are somewhat older than you. They must be in their late teens by now... let me see. Kai is seventeen now and strong. His father says that his basilisk form is white, with glittery red and blue scales down his side. The South Kingdom loves their Prince, for he is honorable and kind. Emot is now fifteen and as swift as the wind, they say. The East Kingdom prides themselves on being so lucky for having such a Prince. His basilisk form is grey with flecks of orange and gold, like the setting sun. Sicrin is nineteen now and smart as a whip. His cleverness is beyond compare. The West Kingdom values intellect most and he is one of the smartest minds there is. His basilisk is jet black with waves of greens and purples."

"Oh, I love purple... Mommy, what color am I?" Maisie was a smart one, and brave to boot.

"Oh, my dear, you were the most beautiful scarlet red when you were born, with swirls of pinks and green. And two very sharp teeth." Clara pretended to bite at Maisie and they both laughed.

Maisie yawned into the room, and Clara tucked her in tighter. "I think it's time for you to get some sleep, Miss Maisie." Clara kissed her head and began to turn out the light.

"Mommy, can you check under the bed for monsters?" I heard the sweet sound of her voice asking.

"Maisie, you know there are no monsters under there. Only the silly old dust bunnies." Her voice was soft in the darkened room, reassuring to a child who thought everything was a story. Her voice conveyed truth. But she lied.

"Kai... ssstay away from the bed." Sicrin hissed in his basilisk form. "Ssshesss asssleeep."

"Ssshut it Sssic. I just want to sssmell her." I couldn't help but work my way farther out from under the bed. The little girl slept peacefully as I explored the room, Sicrin close on my tail. Emot slithered out from under the bed slowly to join Sic and me. I curled around myself in the doorway just as Clara walked by, she knew we watched over Maisie now that she was promised to us. It's a basilisk thing, the males protected their female no matter what age they were. She could be two and we would still protect her every night.

Margaret 'Maisie' Day had no idea we watched over her as she slept. At eight years old we knew we would have to wait until she grew up more before she would be ours; but in the meantime, we would continue to protect her from her father. Maisie tossed in her sleep and began to mumble softly. Sic shifted to stand and padded quietly on bare feet to rub her back. His body casting a shadow over the sleeping girl.

We were the monsters she talked about, the ones who lived under her bed. Little did she know, under her bed was another world entirely. Basilisks were real. We had scales and fangs... jaws that can crush bone... bodies that can squeeze the life out of a person in seconds. Our nest was almost ready for our mate... we just had to wait for her to grow up.

Maisie settled into a deeper sleep and Sic shifted back and curled his massive body on the floor by her bed. Emot and I curled up on the other two sides. We watched as the night passed into day, only to slither under the bed as the dawn approached.

Maisie

"Happy hatch day to you, Happy hatch day to you, Happy hatch day Miss Maisie, Happy hatch day to you." Oh my god, my mom was the devil. She persisted in singing that stupid song every year, but finally, I can leave. Move out on my own and conquer the world. Sam and I had a plan to run away to Vegas and get married just as soon as school gets out in two days. I would be hitting the road and never looking back. Sam didn't know what I was, but I had every intention of living as a human for the rest of my life. If I was not mated by my twenty-first birthday, I would lose my shift permanently. Only three years to go.

"Maisie, Earth to Maisie... you in there?" I couldn't help but flinch nervously. Caught daydreaming about a human life. It didn't help that I was also thinking about last week when Sam and I got caught fucking in the back of his truck by the local cops. Mom was not happy about that one.

"Sorry mom, I'm just excited about graduation." So, what if I lied? I wasn't telling her that I planned to leave. "The cupcakes

Mom set the large cupcake down in front of me and sighed. "Maisie, you really should break up with Sam. I like him, really, I do, but you're promised in marriage to three Princes." she paused momentarily, "I can't stress this enough." I tuned mom out as I peeled the wrapper off my cupcake and shoved it in my mouth whole, so I didn't have to talk.

Mumbling what should have sounded like 'I'm going to be late for school' but really just blew cupcake crumbs everywhere, as garbled noise exited my mouth. Rushing to get ready, I swallowed the cupcake as I changed. As soon as my shoes were on, I grabbed my book bag and hit the ground running. Four more days and Sam and I would be husband and wife.

Two Days Later

Graduation arrived and I made it through the ceremony without falling on my face. Climbing the steps to the stage had been the most nerve-racking experience of my life. Sam and I planned on leaving first thing in the morning and I had my bag packed and ready. I was sneaking out at midnight to meet him and then we would leave this tiny town for a better life. As I climbed the stairs, I began daydreaming about what our life would be like.

Mom was in the kitchen making dinner, so I had half an hour to just put on some music and relax. I opened the door to see three men standing there, all dressed in jeans and t-shirts. I screamed and ran back to the stairs when I heard a familiar sound. The hiss was my mothers, and I could tell she was pissed. She slithered past me into my room, only to shift back just as swiftly when she got there. She began talking as if she knew the three and I couldn't help my curiosity.

I snuck back towards the door and peeked around the corner. All these men were gorgeous. They made Sam look downright plain in comparison. The one in the middle stood six foot four easily, with rock hard muscles that strained the confines of his shirt. His arms were tanned, suggesting he spent a lot of time outdoors. His brown hair had mixes of red and blonde, while his nose was perfectly proportioned to his face. His square jaw gave him the look of a model, but it was his eyes I couldn't look away from. They were crystal blue, like the Caribbean Sea, and they looked decidedly reptilian.

The other two were just as easy on the eyes as the one in the middle. The one to the right, stood about six foot two, blonde hair and just as perfect a face as his buddies; he also wore glasses that made his emerald eyes stand out even more. He was leaner than the other two and his lips looked like they would be good for more than just talking. I ducked back behind the door frame when he caught a glimpse of me, only to hear a deep chuckle that sent chills all the way down to my clit.

I peeked back around after a moment and glanced at the last guy. He had to be six foot five or more. He stood taller than the other two but wasn't as bulky as the middle one. He was lean but not skinny, and his arms still stretched his shirt. He had jet black hair shaved close to the scalp and grey eyes that spoke of secrets whispered in the dark. His face was softer than the other two, and I could see small laugh lines around the edges of his eyes. Those lines deepened as he smiled, and I about fell over at the hint of a fang I saw. His smile was a deadly weapon; it was slightly crooked like he had a secret he would never share.

I slowly walked back down the hall on silent feet until I heard my mom call out. "Margaret Eliza Day get in here right now." Fuck, she used the full name. I turned on my heel and slowly trudged back to my room.

"Yes, mom?" I called softly, as I rounded the doorframe.

"I want to introduce you." She pointed to Blondie first. "This is His Royal Highness, Prince Sicrin Wells." She waited for me to shake his hand. Pointing at Hulk next. "This is His Royal Highness, Prince Kai Harding." I shook Hulk's hand and noticed how it swallowed mine. "This is His Royal Highness, Prince Emot Howe." She finished pointing to Buzzcut.

I went to shake his hand, but he pulled mine to his lips. "The pleasssure, isss all mine," his hiss evident even when he spoke in human form.

"Gentleman, this is my daughter. Her Royal Highness, Princess Margaret Eliza Day." They all bowed, and I about laughed but mom gave me the death stare.

I turned to leave Mom to her company, when she grabbed my arm. Her hiss strong as she whispered to me. "Sssince I know you planned on leaving with Sssam, they have come early to collect you and take you back to Lasssina."

My jaw dropped; I couldn't believe what I just heard. "You can't expect me to leave with these strangers, and I'm not leaving Sam, I love him."

"Oh, please... You only think you love Sam. You're a Basilisk, and you need to mate with another Basilisk," she countered.

"Yeah... so I can then run for my life when one of these three tries to murder me... all because I got pregnant." My mother flinched as if I had slapped her.

"You're leaving tonight, and that's final." I watched her walk out of the room leaving me with these three men. Men I knew nothing about and was suddenly expected to mate.

2

Maisie

Just then my phone rang, and the caller ID said 'Sam'. I slid the button over and answered, "Hello."

"*Hey babe, wanna catch a movie with Ella and Jake tonight?*" he sounded cheerful, the total opposite of how I felt.

"I can't tonight. My mom has guests over and I'm expected to stay," I lied; I couldn't very well tell him the truth.

"*Shit, oh well, maybe after we get settled in Vegas, they can come visit. Love ya, talk later.*" He didn't even wait for my response before hanging up the phone.

I turned around and looked at the three men standing in my room. "So, what am I supposed to do now?" I couldn't help the bitchy tone I had.

"Your mom invited us to stay for dinner, then we pack and leave," Hulk said.

"Ignore Kai, he isn't the best with words... I'm Sicrin, but you can call me Sic. We have been waiting ten years to finally meet you." He smiled softly and his emerald eyes lit from within.

"What do you mean finally meet me?" my tone still bitchy.

Emot spoke up softly, "We're the monstersss under your bed, love... We've been watching over you sssince you were eight." He paused and slapped Sic in the chest. "Hell, this sssofty used to rub your back when you had nightmaresss." Sic blushed but didn't say anything.

Thankfully, Mom yelled up the stairs about dinner. I rushed out as fast as I could just to get away from these weirdos. I vaguely heard a grunt and a hissed 'Ass' as I ran down the stairs.

Dinner was quiet and strained. What did I have to say to anyone? Mom kept up inane conversation, as if she knew these guys well. Hell, if what they said was true, she knew them better than I ever would. I was still planning on sneaking out, only my timetable had been moved up slightly. I plotted my escape to Sam's house as I sat silently, eating my food. These guys seemed nice and all, but I didn't know them. I knew Sam, Sam was safe, and scale-free. I finished my last bite and stood swiftly. Walking my plate to the sink, I rinsed it off and ran back up the stairs. I grabbed my bag and shimmied myself out the window while everyone was still eating. Climbing down the trellis was second nature to me now, as I snuck out regularly to see Sam.

Once my feet hit the ground, I booked it towards the back fence and hopped over. Skirting Mr. Junks pool, I exited out his side gate, before turning up the block towards Sam's. I ran the four blocks 'til I could see his door and slowed. Walking the rest of the way to catch my breath. My hope was that he would be surprised that I'd come early. Skipping up the path to the door, I opened it like always. Stepping into the living room, my vision was assaulted by the view of Sam, naked, with Pamela Conrad bouncing on his cock. I must have made a noise because they

both froze. Turning, I ran, Sam running naked out his door after me. "Maisie, wait!" I heard his yell, but didn't stop until I was back at Mr. Junks house.

I slowly opened his gate and walked through only to stop as I saw all three of my mom's guests, waiting by the fence. I ignored them as I hopped back over said fence and walked to the back door. Just as I opened the glass door my phone buzzed, I looked at the caller ID, 'Sam', I slid the ignore button and turned my phone off. I threw my phone on the table, dropped my bag, and walked up to my room. Slamming the door, I fell face first into the bed and bawled.

I didn't hear the soft knock, and I barely felt the hand rubbing my back as I cried. When Mom came in, she had a box of tissues and my bag. "Maybe now would be a good time to leave." She whispered, I assumed to one of the guys.

The hand paused briefly. "We have time, let her get it out, Clara." The hand continued its motion, rhythmically soothing me.

"If Vago finds her without you three, he will kill her." Mom's voice was muffled by the pillows I had buried my head under, but I knew she was talking about my father.

"We have time Clara, he only arrived yesssterday. From what Sssalima sssaid he landed in New York. It will take him at leassst two daysss to get here," the hissed S's suggested that Emot was speaking.

"I don't want her here if he's coming for her," mom's voice ratcheted up a notch, and I could tell she was worried.

I rose from the pillows and wiped my nose. "Why would he bother coming after me?"

Sic, looked sadly at me. "You became the Queen of all Lasina on your eighteenth birthday. We signed a Treaty with your mother on your eighth birthday, that makes us your Kings. It is not uncommon for females to have multiple mates as there aren't as many females as males. Your birth was the first royal female birth in six hundred years. Your father didn't want to lose his own throne just to unite the Kingdoms, so he tried to kill your mother when he found out you were a girl. We've been looking after you and protecting you since our families signed the Treaty. You were eight, and you used to like us monsters."

I stared in shock; pretty sure I could catch flies in my mouth at the moment. "I'm what... I can't be a Queen... and we aren't married, how can you three be my kings?"

Kai rubbed the back of his neck awkwardly. "Actually, we technically are married. The Treaty was binding in not only the Kingdoms' fate but also all of ours. It basically married us, and to break it would cause a war for all of Lasina."

I gawked at my mother. "Were you ever going to tell me this?" I was yelling by the time the question left my mouth.

"I tried to Maisie, really I did; but how do you tell your daughter she's basically been married since she was eight?" she sounded defeated, lost, and scared.

"Where are we going? Where are we supposed to go to live and what... makes baby basilisks?" I realized my hurt was fading to the background as anger filled me. Anger was so much better than the pain of betrayal... first Sam... and now my mom.

"We have a nest set up back in Lasina... We think you will be pleased with our efforts," Kai spoke up, this time he sounded pleased, as if I would just fall in love with them because of a nest.

"Great, so I'm supposed to live in a nest... like a god damned bird. If you haven't noticed I don't have fucking feathers." I was yelling by the time I was done, and Kai flinched slightly at my tone.

"No, Sugar you don't have feathers... but you do have scales... and our nests aren't like birds' nests. They are not much different than this house, only a lot bigger to accommodate a basilisk's size," Kai's sarcasm was loud and clear as he spoke.

Mom was about to say something when a crash sounded from downstairs. "He's here." She shifted into her basilisk and blocked the door with her massive body, poised to strike at a moment's notice. The guys shifted into formation behind her when she hissed.

Kai's massive bulk dwarfed my mother's form as he slithered his way past her. "Get her packed... We need to leave now... I'll ssstall him." Sic and Emot shifted back to human form, albeit now naked.

I couldn't help but stare at their bodies as they grabbed items and shoved them into a bag. They kept shoving more and more into the bag, until all that was left in my room was the bed. How in the hell had they fit my dresser into a bag no bigger than my backpack? Mom darted forward and shifted, hugging me tightly. "You will always be safe... I promise. I love you, my sweet Maisie." She yelled for Kai and then shifted back into her Basilisk just as Kai came running.

His hair was messy, and he had blood running down his chest. I gasped when I saw the huge bite on his shoulder. "Let's go." I watched in horror as a massive green basilisk slammed into my mom. She fought back swiftly wrapping her body around his and biting everywhere. The green Basilisk roared in pain as she kept up her assault. I stood frozen as he threw her across the

15

room. Kai shifted again and wrapped his large scaly body around mine. Sic and Emot flipped my bed out of the way and Kai darted through a portal I never knew was there. We hurdled towards the ground and I looked up just in time to see the portal close behind Sic and Emot. My scream never stopped as we free fell over thirteen thousand feet without a parachute.

3

Maisie

I'm gonna die, this is the end, I'll be crushed. I noticed Sic and Emot shifting in midair and then Emot was speeding towards us. He had wings, unlike Sic and Kai, small bat-like wings. Kai unwrapped himself from my body and dropped like a stone as Emot's tail wrapped around my waist. I felt our descent slow as the others slammed into the ground.

We floated closer to the ground just as Kai and Sic shifted back to human form. Sic's shoulder looked jacked up and Kai was still bleeding. Emot lowered me gently to the ground and then dropped to shift himself. "Fuck that was close... Can you please relocate this...? I hit a bit wrong this time," Sic asked Emot as he walked closer.

"How are you still alive?" I couldn't believe they had survived such a fall.

Emot jerked Sic's shoulder back into place with a loud pop, and Sic hissed through his teeth. "Normally we open it at ground level, but just like common Earth snakes, we have the ability to fall large distances without injury... most times. Emot has wings, so he could survive a fall twice that distance," as Sic trailed off I realized they were all still naked. Mom always shifted with her clothes on, so why hadn't they?

Kai must have noticed my gaze and he laughed, his cocks rising slightly as if begging for my attention. "We shifted too fast and didn't bother with keeping our clothes on."

I drew my eyes towards the sky and then asked what was upmost in my mind, "Where are we?"

Emot looked around before pointing towards the trees to our east... how I knew it was, was anyone's guess, something about basilisk senses. "That's the eastern border of the Central Lands of Lasina... They were created as a middle ground. Neutral Zone... if you will... but it's all yours. We are about a day from the nest... if we had had more time, we would have opened the portal to the nest itself."

"How do you open portals anyway? Like, can you all do it?" I was curious and hopeful I would be able to get back home soon... I had no intention of staying here in Lasina.

"Only Sic can open portals... each of our breeds has a different trait. The East Kingdom is known for its magical abilities, while in the West Kingdom we can glide on air and are super-fast. The South Kingdom are the strongest of the races... While the North is the most venomous." I looked at the bite marks on Kai's shoulder and noticed beneath the blood, black vein-like tendrils spreading across his skin.

He shifted under my gaze and then Emot handed me the small bag that had my stuff in it. "If we hurry, we might make it to the nest before sunrise... I'll shift and carry everyone, that way we can make good time." Sic pulled me back from Emot as he shifted swiftly. Once shifted, I admired his form. He wasn't the first basilisk I had seen but definitely bigger than my mother, or me, for that matter.

His body was one large mass of muscle, encased in beautifully silky scales. The dying rays of the sun caught the colors and made them sparkle. When he moved, he looked like a living sunset, with golds and oranges all painted on a grey background. The random diamond pattern adding to the overall beauty of his form. He tucked his wings close to his body and slithered closer. I stroked his scales softly and his body rippled under my hand. Sic lifted me up onto Emot's back and hopped up behind me... Kai climbed up in front of me. Once we were settled, Emot took off like a bullet, and the wind tugged at my hair.

The feel of a snake body between my thighs was a new feeling and yet not wholly unpleasant. His muscles flexed and relaxed as he slithered across the open plains towards a massive mountain to the North West... snake senses. We sped through the tall grass nearing the base of the mountain. Emot slowed as we reached the rocky terrain, and began working himself over large rocks carefully, trying not to dislodge us. Kai was slumped forward in between Emot's wings, his breathing shallow.

I screamed as he slowly slid off of Emot's back, Sic jumping after him. Emot stopped and coiled around me, while scoping the terrain. I was wearing a snake like a Snuggie, while watching Sic checking Kai over. Sic looked grimly at Emot. "Go get Salima... Quickly." Emot uncoiled from me and took off into the air like a bullet being fired from a gun, up the mountain. Sic pulled me close to his and Kai's side, placing my hands over Kai's wound to slow the bleeding. "The blood loss is weakening him... the venom he can survive without aid." I had a feeling he was talking to himself as much as me.

"Do you have any bandages?" I was trying to think back to my high school CPR class.

"No, but you might have something we can use in the bag." Sic set my bag on the ground and jumped in feet first,

disappearing from view. Night was setting in and a chill filled the air as I put pressure in Kai's bite wound. Sic climbed back out with what looked like a shirt and handed it over. I took the shirt and placed it under my hands not caring which shirt I just ruined. I pressed down and heard Kai hiss in pain, as I pressed harder using my body weight for all it was worth.

I was beginning to think Kai would die while we waited for Emot to return. The sky turned dark as we waited, and Kai had passed out completely, when I finally heard the sound of wings. Emot and several other winged basilisks landed next to our spot. A tall slender woman jumped off Emot's back and rushed over to Kai, pushing me out of the way in the process. Sic pulled me away as the woman began using magic to seal Kai's wounds. The other four basilisks stood guard around us as she worked her magic. Once Kai's wounds were sealed a guard scooped him up and took off flying towards the top of the mountain.

A second and third guard scooped up Sic and Salima taking off as well. The last guard stood watching as Emot shifted just the top half of his body into human form and picked me up behind the knees. I was cradled close to his chest; his heart beat loud in my ear. "Hold on tight," he commanded, and I wrapped my arms around his neck. We took off from the ground and were flying high in seconds. The last guard swiftly falling behind.

"Why didn't we just fly to the nest if you're so fast," I had to yell over the wind rushing by.

We caught up to the other guards and even Kai before he answered. "I can't fly while carrying three people. One yesss, three no. My wings can only handle so much extra weight." I felt stupid for asking, I should have realized.

Within moments, I began to see the silhouette of a large castle. The lights from several rooms gave it a fairytale quality,

20

and I couldn't help but be impressed by the sheer size. Emot slowed as we approached, dropping gracefully in a large courtyard filling with guards in both human and basilisk form. Emot set me down gently and shifted back to his fully human form, a guard rushed over with a robe for him. I watched as he wrapped himself in the silk robe and tied the belt.

He pulled me towards the door just as the rest of the guards arrived with the others. A stretcher was brought out and Kai was laid on it before being rushed in through the main doors, and deeper into the castle. Salima rushed after him just as her feet touched the ground. Sic was handed a robe similar to Emot's and then the guards went back to their posts. Sic held out an arm for me and escorted me through the massive front entry.

"Welcome to our nest, Margaret," his words were proud, and yet I could hear a tinge of worry, like he truly cared what I thought of this place.

"It's beautiful..." It truly was a beautiful sight, but I had no intention of staying here in Lasina, so I don't know why he cared about my opinion. "Is Kai going to be alright?" I was feeling guilty because I was the reason he was hurt.

"I'll take you to see him after you get settled into your room." Sic pulled me up a grand staircase, that curved up the left side of the hall. The castle was reminiscent of the Salzburg High Fortress from the sixteenth century, only much larger and with nicer finishes inside. The history geek in me loved the idea of living in here. However the rest of me wanted nothing more than to be fully human, and invisible.

We stopped at a grand pair of double doors at the top of the stairs and Emot threw them wide open. Sic escorted me into the massive sitting room with a cheery fire in a massive grate. There was a TV above the fireplace and Sic pointed to it. "We

don't get cable or anything, but we have Blu-ray and video games from our trips to Earth." I walked around looking over the furnishings, comfy couches and chairs were spread everywhere. A bookshelf filled with books sat by a bay window.

Across the room stood another set of large doors. Sic opened them when he noticed me looking at them. The largest bed I had ever seen, stood directly in the center of a massive bedroom. "Holy shit, how many people can that bed fit?" I couldn't help but gawk at the massive thing.

Emot chuckled behind me and I jumped at his closeness. "I would sssay in human form a dozen, but in basssilisssk form... Maybe five, if they are all tangled together," he whispered the last part into my ear suggestively, painting a picture of sin in my brain.

"Those doors lead to the bathroom," Sic pointed, as he pulled me farther into the room.

"And what about those doors?" I pointed to four doors that sat opposite the bathroom.

"Those are our rooms," just as he spoke, Salima walked out of the second door down and towards us.

4

Emot

I watched Salima walk towards us and prayed to Jörmungandr, the Norse snake we all descended from; I prayed he would be alright. Salima was covered in Kai's blood and she looked exhausted.

"He will live. I gave him an elixir to stop the poison, and his wounds are healed but he will be weak for several days, from blood loss. I got him cleaned up so you can see him." She kissed Sic on the cheek and began to walk away.

"Thank you, Sssalima," I called before she exited. She nodded to me but kept walking.

Maisie arched a questioning brow at Sic and he blushed some. "She's my mom," was all he replied, causing her eyebrows to raise higher.

I left them to do whatever and rushed into Kai's room. He was lying in bed covered in nothing but a sheet. His eyes looked heavy, but he was awake. "Man, you look like ssshit," I commented, as I sat next to him on the bed.

He grunted a laugh and then groaned, "I feel like shit."

"Can I get you anything?" His hand lifted to point at the nightstand.

"Water would be nice, or maybe a bottle of vodka to wash the foul taste of Salima's elixir out of my mouth." I couldn't help but laugh at his comment as I reached for the glass. I helped him sit up some so he could drink, and then replaced the glass on the nightstand. "So, does she like the place?" his question was soft.

"I think ssshe does, ssshe sssaid it was beautiful… but I don't think ssshe plans on ssstaying if you want my honessst opinion." Kai and I told each other everything, he was my best friend, and more.

"What makes you say that?" he asked scooting over slowly to give me more room.

I laid down next to him and stared off at the ceiling. "Just a feeling, I guesss. Ssshe wassn't happy when we pulled her through the portal… I don't think ssshe ever planned on coming home."

I felt his hand grasp mine and squeeze softly. "We will just have to convince her to stay."

A knock sounded on the door before it opened, and Sic walked in. "Maisie's in the shower. How are you feeling?"

"Like I got run over by a herd of centaurs, and that fucking sucks. I should know." He did know… last year he was run over by a herd while visiting the Jotnar on the continent of Manden. I didn't know much about our world but Sic did, and I was fairly sure he would be rhapsodic in telling Maisie all about the home she came from and likely didn't know.

"Emot doesn't think Maisie will stay," Kai mentioned as Sic leaned against the bedpost.

"Why do you think that?" Sic asked, seemingly not worried in the slightest.

I looked over at him. "Ssshe fully intended to run away with that guy... she wasssn't planning on coming here. Now that ssshe'sss here, I just have a feeling ssshe will leave at the first chance."

Sic ran his hand through his hair like he always did when thinking. "Maybe she just needs to be shown the benefits of living here. Show her around the Kingdoms. She just found out she's a Queen and is for all intents and purposes, married to us. Adjusting is going to take time." He stood up. "Come on Emot, let's let Kai get some rest... we can talk about this in the morning."

I watched him walk out the door leaving it open for me. I scooted towards the edge of the bed when Kai groaned. "What? No good night kiss for the invalid, first Sic now you... damn cold man."

I leaned over and pecked him on the mouth swiftly. "Better? Don't let the humansss under the bed get you," I couldn't help but tease, as I walked towards the door.

"Hardly asshole. Have a good night," Kai already sounded like he was drifting off. I closed the door softly and walked to the living room. Sic was sitting at the window looking out into the dark.

I flopped down on the far side and waited. I knew he would start talking eventually, if I just waited quietly. I didn't have to wait long. "Do you really think she will run?"

"I think all of thisss is a big change for her... We also don't know if Clara survived. Ssshe might want to know if her mother isss alive or dead. I jussst think we need to be prepared for the

eventuality, that ssshe could run," I couldn't help but point out the facts. Maisie was in a new world for fuck sake, she would need time to adjust and realistically speaking, she might never adjust.

I heard the door open and Maisie walked into the sitting room. Her wet hair dripping down her back. I had been watching her during the nights for ten years now, but this view was a thousand times better. Her heart-shaped face was creamy in completion, her nose perfectly straight, her lips full and utterly kissable. She was small compared to us, maybe five foot five. We had all watched her grow from a gangly child to a curvaceous beauty. I had to adjust myself as I noticed her hardened nipples peeking through her shirt, her long hair wetting the fabric, making it almost transparent.

She walked over to the fireplace and sat on the rug to brush her hair. Basilisks in general loved to be warm, even in the height of summer we had a fire going. In this, Maisie was all basilisk. She spoke up from the rug, as we sat by the window, "So, tell me more about this place. Whose castle is it? And where is this nest you spoke of?"

I laughed at her questions until I got punched in the arm by Sic. He stood and walked over to sit on the couch in front of the fire. I composed myself and joined him on the sofa as Maisie stared at us, waiting for whatever we had to say.

"This is our castle, more specifically, your castle. This is the nest we were speaking about," Sic's words had my mouth gaping. I looked at Emot, but he just shrugged and nodded, confirming what Sic had said.

"This... palace... is mine? How? I've never been to Lasina before. How can I have a palace? This has to be a joke." I couldn't believe what I was hearing.

Sic smiled softly. "It's not a joke. We started building it when the Treaty was signed. Kai, Emot, and I placed every stone in this palace. We just finished it about two years ago." I was stunned, they had built this place just for me. "This is your nest. I don't know how much you know about basilisk culture, seeing as you were raised as a human, but males build a nest for their mate. Since you are a Queen, we were required to build a castle. We based it off a castle in Austria, your mother said it was your favorite when you visited there." I could see the influence in the way the castle was structured but the inside was vastly more modern.

"It's a beautiful castle." I didn't know what else to say... It wasn't home so it didn't feel like mine. "I guess I'll head to bed.

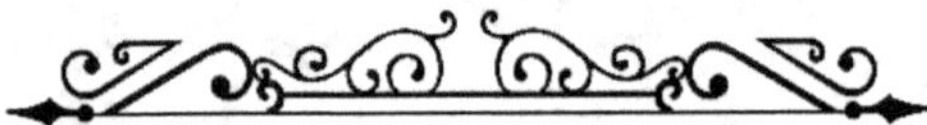

Where are you two going to sleep?" I was worried they would say with me.

"We have our own rooms, just like Kai does. We won't be far if you need anything." Sic pointed towards the room. I was relieved they didn't expect to sleep with me.

"Well... goodnight then." I stood and walked towards the door, leaving the two alone. I closed the door and climbed into the massive bed, crawling across its expanse to sleep in the center. I piled pillows all around me and curled up into a ball letting the stress and emotions of the day wash through me. I felt tears begin to slide down my cheeks as everything came crashing down on me. I cried myself to sleep.

I spun around just in time to see my mom's body hit the wall. Her neck punctured by two massive holes. She crumpled to the floor in a pool of blood, and I screamed. Vago turned his attention towards me, an eerie smiled spreading across his face. "I have you now bitch. You won't take my Kingdom from me," His words were hissed and menacing.

I felt his tail wrap around my throat squeezing off my oxygen. I did the only thing I could think to do, and I shifted.

"Holy fuck. Maisie wake up." My eyes flew open, but they weren't my human eyes. I had shifted at some point in my sleep and was now coiled around Sic's naked body, his very human and turning blue body. I swiftly uncoiled and he gasped for breath. "What happened?" was all he asked, once he caught his breath.

"I don't know. I had a nightmare. Vago killed my mom, then wasss trying to kill me." This was why I hated the snake form, the lisp.

Sic reached out a hand a stroked my scales alongside my neck. My body responded without warning and my muscles relaxed. I felt myself shifting back into human form, only to realize I was just as naked as Sic was. I pulled the sheet over me as fast as possible, but he still got a good look.

"Do you want me to get you anything? Or stay with you for a while?" Sic's words were kind, implying he would stay to keep me company if, and only if, I wanted him to.

"No thank you. I think I'll go sit by the fire for a bit, try to calm down, maybe grab a book." I waited for Sic to leave, only he stayed; his leg bent up blocking my view of his junk. Blushing, I turned away to give him a moment. The bed dipped as he rose, and his footsteps headed towards his own room. His ass was the only thing to capture my gaze as his door softly clicked shut.

Looking around the empty room, I climbed my way off the bed, finding a robe to wear. I padded barefoot to the sitting room and noticed an odd shimmer across the sky through the window. It danced to and fro, painting a beautiful pallet of colors with each pass. Walking closer to the window, I curled up on the window seat to watch the show.

An undetermined amount of time passed as I watched the swirling lights, but I was startled out of my thoughts by Kai, as he walked closer near. "They are beautiful, aren't they?"

"Shouldn't you be in bed still?" I watched as he worked himself into a comfy position across the window from me.

He shrugged softly. "Those two are being loud and when I went to go tell them to shut the fuck up... I noticed you weren't in bed. So, I came looking for you." He looked out the window at the lights and sighed. "They always remind me of home. The South kingdom has a closer view of them."

"What are they? I've been mesmerized for... I don't even know how long." I looked over to see Kai's soft smile.

"They are the Mer lights... Mermaids that live in the South Sea. They are very different from fairy tale mermaids though. Last time I saw one, a dead male had washed up on the shore. Their tails are bioluminescent, and they come to the surface at night, casting light into the sky like a spotlight of sorts. Atlantis is protected by shields that only a Mer can go through, and they have the ability to shift into the human form. They aren't friendly with most species here, they do tolerate us though," he paused in his speech and looked at me sheepishly. "Sorry, I used to watch them every night as a kid, it's been a long time since I've enjoyed their magic."

I looked back out the window to see more colors join the tapestry of the sky. "Why has it been a while since you've gotten to see them?"

He looked over at me and chuckled, "Once the Treaty was signed, and you were officially ours, we spent our nights on Earth protecting you. We slept on the floor in your room every night, from the time you were eight until last night."

My jaw dropped. "Every night, like every, every night?" All I could think about was all the times I had snuck Sam into my room late at night, and we would have sex before he snuck back out.

"Oh yes, sugar, every night... not one missed. Although we tried to stay hidden most nights." His grin showed me he knew why I asked. "Are you embarrassed to know we were there all the time?"

"A bit, to think you guys could see me having sex is a bit embarrassing." I could feel my cheeks heating at the idea.

"For what it's worth, we couldn't exactly see. The portal was under your bed, so it lacked a vantage point, but we could hear... and from what I heard, he wasn't doing the greatest of jobs. But you already knew that." He smirked before continuing on, "I will say hearing that vibrator after he left was the hardest to deal with."

I gaped like a fish at his words and he had the gall to laugh. "Oh, come now sugar, admit that you would have rather had a man than a little boy." I was flabbergasted, floored, utterly dumbfounded... but didn't know if it was because he was right, or because he was mentioning it at all.

"If it makes you feel better, those nights sucked for us too. It's not easy hearing your mate enjoy another man when you can't enjoy another woman's company. Don't get me wrong, we made do with each other, but it's not the same." Did he just say what I thought he said?

"You mean you guys haven't had sex in ten years?" I honestly didn't believe it.

"Oh no, you misunderstand. We've had plenty of sex, just not with any females. When you're royalty and technically married, there is no female in Lasina willing to touch you. Before the Treaty, yes, anyone who could, tried; after though, we only had each other." I understood the aspect of them not having any other woman but what did he mean by only each other.

Curiosity got the better of me. "What do you mean by you only had each other?" He shifted uncomfortably before looking me in the eyes.

"I mean that the only two people I've had sex with in ten years are currently in that room there." He pointed towards the doorway to the bedrooms.

"Like in human form, like anal?" I blurted out before I could stop myself.

He laughed, only this time it was a hardy belly laugh that sent tingles across my skin. "Among other ways, yes. It's not uncommon, even among the human population, correct?"

"No, you're right, it is common. What do you mean other ways, how else do two guys have sex?" I was fully engrossed into this conversation, and I didn't know why, but I was intrigued.

"What all do you know about basilisk biology? Male versus female." I looked at him like he was the biggest moron.

"Males have a penis, and women a vagina. What else is there?" I laughed as I said my answer.

"Well firstly, I'm not talking about human anatomy but basilisk anatomy. Secondly, male basilisks have two penises, in both forms, we can also have one penis in human form. They can combine when in human form, to become one very impressive appendage, I might add. Thirdly, when in basilisk form, they remain inverted in our body cavity until sexually aroused; this creates a canal very similar to a vagina. Let's just say they don't feel all that different either. So, to answer your question, we do have sex in human form, normal anal sex; however, we can also have sex in basilisk form if one remains inverted while the other is aroused, most of the time we do it that way in a half shifted state, hands are always an added benefit." He stopped talking, probably because of the look on my face.

I had so many questions I didn't even know where to begin. "So, like what if the one who is basically the penis fly trap gets aroused. Is it like a cock in that it gets erect? Does it push the other cocks out? How can you walk with two penises? Do you have four balls as well? If one cock gets hard does the other, or do

32

they work independently of each other? Does one hang to the left, and one to the right when you're wearing pants?" Questions shot out rapid fire, just as quickly as my brain thought them up.

"Breathe sugar, I'll answer all the questions you might have. Or maybe just show you." Kai stood and held out his hand to help me stand. I hesitantly placed mine in his and he pulled me off the window seat and against his body. He ground his hips against mine and I felt two distinct shafts side by side. "Wanna see?" He whispered softly in my ear.

I stepped back quickly and looked at the ceiling. "Maybe some other time. I think I'll leave my questions unanswered until the morning." I bolted for the bedroom, Kai's husky laugh following me even after I closed the door.

6

Maisie

I walked into the bedroom just as Sic walked out of his room, or was that Emot's room? He just so happened to be stark naked with two cocks. I couldn't help but gape as he rushed back into the room and slammed the door. Okay, Kai wasn't joking about having two cocks. I also had my question about balls answered as I only saw two. Kai walked up behind me in the doorway and then pushed me slowly to the bed. Once there, he pulled the covers back and then walked towards his own door. "Good night, sugar," was all he said, as he closed his door.

I climbed into bed still digesting what exactly I saw, and surprisingly how turned on I was. Sic's cocks, plural, were both more than Sam had, I could only imagine what they looked like combined. I faced away from the doors, just in case, and tried to fall back asleep. My mind wouldn't calm down though as everything rushed through my mind once again. I dozed off just as sunlight began pouring in through the windows behind the bed. I was vaguely aware of the guys closing curtains around the bed, encasing me in the pitch blackness that allowed me to fall into a deep sleep.

I woke to the sound of voices in the outer room, as Kai and Sic argued about something. I crawled to the end of the bed and fumbled sleepily to the door. I opened them wide only to have four faces swing my way. Three of which looked on in horror as they jumped up to stand in front of me. Sic pulled my robe back into position before they stepped back. The fourth guy stood by the couch facing the ceiling to give us privacy.

"What is going on? What are you arguing about?" I yawned as I asked, making my words garbled.

"We are sssorry for waking you, but my father came to meet you and tell us the newsss," Emot spoke softly.

"What news, is everything alright?" It was still too early for me and I just wanted to pass back out, but if they had a visitor this early it must be important.

"Come sit and Evat can fill you in." Sic held out his arm and I blushed slightly when I placed my hand on it. My mind was filled with images from last night, and snippets of the conversation Kai and I had. He walked me to the couch, but I sat on the floor in front of the roaring fire instead. "Evat, this is Maisie. Maisie, this is Emot's father, Evat."

Evat bowed his head towards me in greeting. "It is nice to finally meet you, young lady. May I say, you are as beautiful as your mother was at your age." His smile was kind like Emot's, only he was older.

"It's nice you meet you... You knew my mother?" I asked softly, curious about a past she had never spoken of often.

"I did actually, I almost wed her, but she fell in love with Vago and asked to be let out of our arranged marriage. I met my wife a few weeks later and a year after Emot was born." He smiled kindly at me, and then turned back to the guys. "He hasn't returned yet... but it's only a matter of time before he does. The issue remains, and the three of you must ensure the Treaty is upheld, to the tee." With those cryptic words, Evat stood. "My dear, it was a pleasure, please feel free to visit the East Kingdom any time." With that, he strolled out the main door and I saw two guards close the door behind him.

"What does he mean by the Treaty must be upheld to a tee?" I watched all three men look sheepishly around at my question.

"The Treaty specifies things we have to do within an allotted time. If we fail to do so the Treaty can be broken by any of the four Kingdoms," Sic was the first to speak up, but I was no closer to understanding it all.

"Where is the Treaty? I want to see it." I needed to know exactly what I was getting myself into, and why. I also needed to know if it was worth running away from.

"Salima has a copy I believe. I will go get her and have her bring her copy for you to go over," Sic stood as he spoke, then he was following Evat out the same doors.

Emot and Kai made small talk, while I sat by the fire gazing at the flames. Sic and Salima returned faster than I expected with a slim folder. Once Salima was seated, Sic handed me the file and I flipped it open on my lap.

Declaration of Peace and Unity.

Recalling the purposes and principles of the Charter of Lasina,

Acknowledging a union between His Royal Highness, Prince Sicrin Wells, His Royal Highness, Prince Kai Harding, His Royal Highness, Prince Emot Howe, Duke of Northplane, Lord Zugo Carmichael, to Her Royal Highness, Princess Margaret Eliza Day. On this day of September 13th 4990 AS.

I paused in reading the very long looking document and looked at Salima. "4990 AS? What does the AS stand for?"

"After the separation. This September 13th marked the 5000th year of our four Kingdoms being apart. The Elders will know the most if you have questions." Salima smiled, encouraging me to continue reading.

This document states that within the First year of marriage after the Princesses eighteenth human birthday, all concerned parties must engage in sexual congress to solidify their union.

My eyes bulged as I glanced back at Salima, but she just continued to smile patiently. I looked back at the papers in my lap and continued.

This document also encourages offspring to be produced at the earliest convenience, however, one cannot mandate the natural body, and therefore, one only encourages.

If the union is deemed void by a lack of congress with any one partner, any nation has the authority to withdrawal from the contract and proceed with the war that has plagued our nation for 5000 years.

His Royal Highness, Prince Sicrin Wells:

Sicrin Wells

His Royal Highness, Prince Kai Harding:

Kai Harding

His Royal Highness, Prince Emot Howe:

Emot Howe

Duke of Northplane, Lord Zugo Carmichael:

Zugo Carmichael

Signing for Her Royal Highness, Princess Margaret Eliza Day; Her Majesty, Queen Clara Ann Day:

Clara Ann Day

Addendum: If any one party is not alive after the Princess reaches her eighteenth birthday, another

suitable candidate will be found to replace the aforementioned member.

I couldn't believe what I was reading, and yet it was in black and white with signatures and everything. My own mother had signed my life away to four men without even consulting me. Granted, I was eight when this was signed but I should have had some say.

I skimmed back over the document several times when something occurred to me. There was a fourth man mentioned and only three here. Where was the fourth? "Who is Zugo Carmichael? Why isn't he here?"

Salima sighed, but took the folder from me and began to explain. "Zugo, is a high lord of the North Kingdom. Unrelated to you by blood or marriage, the Elders felt every nation should be represented since you were not raised on Lasina. They believed your Earthly upbringing would create a neutrality that was needed to join all the nations together. The only nation who hasn't embraced this peace has been the North. Your father imprisoned Zugo when he heard about his role in the Treaty. Last we heard, Zugo was still being held captive in the northern mountains," she paused briefly, and looked at the guys one by one. "Your first duty to your new Queen is to rescue him. You all know this." She looked me dead in the eye. "And your first duty before they leave is to consummate the union."

I blushed to the roots of my hair, I hated talking about sex with adults... oh wait I'm technically an adult. Fine, with adultier adults. "How can you expect me to sleep with people I know nothing about? I just met these three, I can't go jumping into the sack with them," indignation won out over my shyness as I spoke, my word getting louder.

"Not to be rude my dear and speaking from experience. You have your entire life to get to know these men. It is not our place to know them before we wed them, that is for those who aren't royalty." I gapped at her in shock, she was blatantly telling me to fuck them, and then get to know them.

"I'm not going to sleep with anyone I don't know, let alone don't love. Contract be damned." She barked a laugh in my face.

"What a lovely childish sentiment, but unfortunately for you, one that cannot apply. If you don't solidify your union before your nineteenth birthday, then all of Lasina will be at war. You don't have time for love, at least not yet," her words were snide, and yet I could hear the truth in them. I decided I was done with this conversation and stood.

"Thank you for allowing me to see the contract no one thought to see if I was alright with. Have a wonderful day." I pulled myself up to my full height of five foot five and walked proudly out of the room.

I leaned against the bedroom door and listened as Sic spoke with his mother, "You don't have to be rude mom. You could have explained it to her much better."

"She needs to understand all that is at stake. She's still a child in all the ways that matter, and she knows nothing of our world," Salima's words were not said unkindly, just a statement of fact.

I walked away from the door and sat on the bed facing the window. The sky was a pale lavender offsetting a crimson sun. Away in the distance, I could see gold waters sparkling in the light. I didn't know if they were from the sea or a nearby lake, but I had the sudden desire to be away from this castle and these men.

7

Maisie

I found the bag that had my stuff on a side table and reached into it for clothes. I couldn't feel anything, so I stuck my head in and a light popped on. The bag was utterly empty. "Where's my stuff?" I yelled to no one and anyone.

Kai opened the door slowly. "What did you yell?"

I turned holding up the bag in my hand. "Where is my stuff?" I accused him, as I shook the bag.

"Oh," he walked towards a door near the bathroom and opened it slowly. "This is your closet, we put all your things away in here. Along with a few other things you might need."

"You unpacked my things? Why would you do that?" I wasn't staying here, not for one more minute. I marched through the doors and drew up short. The closet was massive, all my furniture was in place with racks, and rack of shoes and clothes. I was more than a bit shocked at the sheer volume of items.

"We've been planning this for ten years, we made sure you would want for nothing here. Emot picked out hundreds of pairs of shoes, while Sic worked on the dresses and other lady things. I made sure you had jeans and t-shirts since that's what you wore

most back in the Earthly realm," his words were soft next to my ear, and I shivered at his nearness.

"Why would you all agree to this? It's utterly ridiculous, not to mention this mysterious fourth man that hasn't been seen in ten years. I'm being set up to fail, so why bother? I want to go home. NOW!" I was venting all my anger, and deep down I knew Kai wasn't deserving of this, but he was the only one here.

"If you go home now, you run the risk of Vago finding and killing you. You are the one piece of the puzzle that is utterly irreplaceable. Sic, Emot, Zugo, and me; we are all replaceable in the Treaty. Hell, I have five brothers that could just as easily take my place. There is no other female royal in all of Lasina that can replace you. Please stay, at least until we get Zugo, or until we hear that Vago is back," he ended his words on a plea for my safety.

"That's a dick move on your part, but fine I'll stay until we hear Vago has returned. Why do you all have similar names? Letter wise at least." I was curious about them at least a tiny bit. He did have a point though, it was smarter to stay until Vago returned, then I would be safe in the Earthly realm. "Can I at least leave this castle?"

"As far as leaving the castle is concerned you will need a guard detail, but yes, you can leave. The names are as old as the split, at least in terms of what they start with. East got A through G, South got H through M, West got N through T, and the North got U through Z. Your grandmother was from the East, your grandfather the West, your father the North, and your mother was born in the South. That is why your family have never stayed within the required lettering mandates. You were born on Earth, and not subject to the customs of our world." Holy crap, they even divided up the alphabet in this world.

I pushed Kai gently back out of the door, my hands resting on his rock-hard chest. Holy shit, the man was a brick encased in gorgeous skin. "Thanks for the lesson, I'm going to dress now, and you can leave." I closed the door on his smiling face, after pushing him back over the threshold.

I turned around and was blown away all over again. So many clothes and shoes my teenage heart was about to burst. I walked along each wall flicking through the countless hangers until I came upon a pair of faded jeans and a cute moon shirt, that said glow in the dark. I pulled open the drawers and found hundreds of panties, all lace or silk, some missing bits in the crotch. Sic was, well, sick, if he thought I would ever wear crotchless panties.

I rummaged through the drawer, throwing things to the floor, until I found a pair of regular cotton underwear with a matching cotton bra. Stripping off the robe I was wearing, I slipped into the comfy white cotton. Then slid perfectly fitting jeans on and pulled the shirt over my head. I found my old worn-out shoes and slipped them on without socks.

I pulled the door open and all three men were standing there waiting in silence. Emot looked at Sic who just smiled, "Kai mentioned you wanted to go out. Is there any particular place you would like to go to? We would be glad to escort you as well as the guards." I sighed, I wanted to get away from them but how was I supposed to tell them that?

"I saw something gold through that window," I pointed to the far window. "I think it's a lake, I want to go there. Alone, if possible." I walked around the line they made in the doorway and opened the bedroom door. I paused and rolled my eyes at the two dozen armed men and women standing at attention in the main room. "Oh, come on, surely I don't need this many guards."

I looked back over my shoulder at the guys, and Sic stepped forward. "If we went with you the detail would be slightly less."

While he was talking, a servant arrived. "Your Majesties, the carriage is ready."

"Seriously, no cars? A freaking carriage. How far is it and why can't I just walk?" I waited for an answer, but no one volunteered one. "Fine, let's go."

The guys followed me out of the room steering me towards the front courtyard but still letting me lead. Guards opened the front door and I skid to a stop at what I saw waiting by the doors. "HOLY SHIT!" I looked over my shoulder at Sic. "Are those freaking unicorns?"

He smiled as the sound of hooves reached my ears. "Yes, they are. They left the Earthly realm to take refuge here. They are the closest thing to horses we have, unless you count the hellhound army brigade. Or the asshole Pegasus shifters."

I gaped at his words. "Hellhounds?"

"Yes, they are actually quite easy to tame, and because of their massive size, they make for an excellent cavalry," he explained but I was still gawking at all black unicorns with silver and gold swirled horns. That is, until the guards surrounding us began mounting the massive beasts, that looked like vicious dogs, the size of elephants.

One rider even cooed over his hellhound and it lolled its massive black tongue out and yipped. Their fur looked like spikes and their bodies were covered in metal plates. Once the guard was mounted, Sic opened the carriage door and helped me inside. "Would you rather have us come?"

"No, I need some space, a few moments alone to catch my breath. I'm sure I'll be fine with all this." I waved my hand to indicate the massive number of hellhounds and guards. Sic closed the door and tapped on the roof twice, there was the crack of a whip, and we smoothly rocked into motion.

Sigrin

I knew the moment I saw her climb in that carriage that she would try to run, that's why her guard detail had been so large. Half to protect her, half to keep her from running. The lake wasn't far by carriage, only half an hour. So, I hoped nothing happened so close to the nest.

"What now asshole?" Kai slapped me on the arm.

"I guess, while we wait for her to run, and fail, and come back... we plan. We need to get the most up-to-date intel on Zugo. If he's still a captive or if he's been turned by Vago. We also need to find the safest route over the wall. Past the armed guards and into wherever he is being kept. Last time was a disaster, and Emot almost died." I could still see the scar on Emot's chest from our last attempt to break Zugo out, when in human form.

Once Clair had left, while still pregnant with Maisie, Vago had built a wall thirty feet tall around his lands and ruled them with tyrannical fervor. No one was allowed in or out, and that included the Duke. The only reason his signature was on there was thanks to a very brave wind runner from the East. They had met in secret, and he had signed.

From what she told us, he wanted out, but she hadn't been strong enough to carry him. He used his own blood and venom to sign the paper, as a sign to how committed he was to the unification of Lasina. He had disappeared several months after he signed the Treaty. He had never seen Maisie, never watched her like we had, and hadn't been able to help build the nest.

We had tried to find him several times but after the last time, we decided to wait until we had Maisie. "Maybe if we use her status we can get in, and get him out. With Vago gone, they won't have anyone in charge," Emot suggested, as we walked towards the great hall. Five thrones were lined up, side by side. The largest one in the center for Maisie.

I sat on the steps leading up to the dais and looked up at Kai and Emot. "Are you really willing to risk her like that? Let's contact our spies and the network within the North Kingdom and go from there." As the oldest, they tended to look to me for command, but once Maisie fully gained her crown, she would be leading us all.

"No, you're right. We shouldn't risk her like that, maybe if we can get word to him that she's here, if he's not imprisoned, then he can meet us at a rendezvous point," Kai spoke up first, "Then we can have the winged guards help fly him back over." I thought about that plan but there were still too many ifs.

"I still think our first course of action should be to find him. Then figure out a rescue plan." I stood and called to a servant standing along the wall. "Find me Viper and tell her the Kings request her presence." It was the first time I had used that term and it rolled awkwardly off my tongue.

"Yes, Your Majesty." He bowed quickly and sped off.

"Are you sure you want Viper? She's the deadliest assassin in Lasina. What is she going to be able to do?" Emot asked, while he looked at me with wide eyes.

"She's also from the North and knows the terrain better than anyone. She can still slip in and out where no one else can. Why I never thought to use her before is a mystery to me." I sighed at my own stupidity for not using her years ago.

"Let's go get food. I'm starved." As always, Kai's appetite overran his brain and he walked off towards the kitchens without waiting for us to follow. Emot and I exchanged a look and followed, as we talked more about the plan.

Maisie

We rolled through a short mountain trail that eventually opened up into a picturesque meadow. Wildflowers, in a rainbow of colors, painted the entire area around the golden lake. The door opened as the guard helped me down, and I walked towards the mesmerizing waters. The light danced across the ripples, giving the water a rose gold hue as it moved.

I stood by the bank and just breathed in the sights. I saw bubbles begin to rise from the center of the lake and stepped back as a giant tentacle reached into the sky only to slam down in the shallows. Walking along the massive suckers, were beautiful people no bigger than a coffee pot. I had to bend down to see them fully, and fully I saw them in all their nakedness.

The one in the lead stopped and bowed to me. Four more began to walk across the suckers holding a beautiful crown of ice. They held it out for me, and the man mimed me putting it on. I reached towards it just as a guard snatched my wrist. "They are Nymphs, Your Majesty," her voice was soft as if trying to not offend.

"I don't care, they clearly wish me to put it on." I snatched my hand away and reached again for the crown.

Once I placed the cold ice on my head the lead man spoke. "Your Majesty of the Basilisk people, we greet you. I am the King of the Nymphs, and these are my Queens." He gestured towards the rows and rows of women along one side of the tentacle. "I have come to bid you welcome, and in a show of good faith, offer you my son as a consort to further goodwill." I tried to hold back a giggle as another tiny man stepped up next to the king. Several wails accompanied his movement.

"Your Majesty, while I appreciate the gesture. I feel your son is of better service to your Kingdom. However, to sow seeds of friendship, you and your consorts would be most welcome to join us for a feast." That should keep Sic, Kai, and Emot busy while I escaped.

He bowed graciously at my offer. "I shall accept and give you time to organize this feast. I will return here in one week for the details. If you ever have need of us just toss a large rock into the lake and Harvey will bring us up to you." He rubbed the tentacle softly and it rippled under his hand. I watched as he held out his palms. "The crown is our only way to communicate with other kinds, so, I shall need to have it back." I slowly took off the crown and placed it softly on to the closest sucker. It swiftly closed around the ice and then the Nymphs all waved as the tentacle lowered back into the water.

"Well, that was strange," I said out loud.

"What is, Your Majesty?" the same guard asked, as I rose back up to stand.

"He offered me his son as a consort." I giggled outright now that they were gone. "Oh, and they are coming to dinner soon." I rushed out that last part.

"Why did you not accept his son as consort? It is a great honor and they are reputed lovers," she was genuinely asking why I didn't accept a six-inch-tall man as a consort.

"He's six inches tall." I continued to laugh.

"In his true form, yes, but Nymphs, like some other creatures here, can alter their size when necessary. They go to the human realm from time to time to breed new blood into their genetic line," she continued to ramble as I looked on in shock at her explanation. She sounded as knowledgeable as Sic, when she began going on about genetics.

"Ok, I get it, I'll talk to the guys and go from there," I said just to shut her up. I began walking around the lake as the sun began to set. I was almost to the tree line in the distance, when a hellhound let out a ghostly howl, that sent chills up my spine. The guards were surrounding me within seconds and the carriage was pulled closer. They swiftly swept me back up to the cushioned seats and then we were racing back to the castle. "Damn, so close," I said to the darkness descending over the landscape we passed.

The sky changed from lavender to a deep violet color, that almost looked black, as we raced back to the castle. This trip seemed to speed by faster than our outgoing one; before I realized it, we were pulling to a stop outside the main doors. A guard opened my door and then escorted me into the castle. The great hall was empty when I entered, but a servant rushing by stopped to bow, giving me the opportunity to ask, "Where are the Princes?"

"They are in the kitchen, Your Majesty. If you follow me, I'll take you there." With that he rushed out a side door, leaving me to follow. We walked down a winding set of stairs into a large open room. It felt like I had stepped into a large-scale restaurant

kitchen, with the newest appliances on the Earthly market. Emot was commanding cooks left and right while wearing a white chef's coat. Sic and Kai sat at a small table drinking a bottle of wine and eating what looked to be an appetizer of sorts.

I couldn't help but watch, as Emot added brandy to his pan and then flambéed whatever was inside. He plated the still flaming pan and placed it on the table by the guys and pulled out a chair. "Dig in fellasss." I watched him douse the flames with lemon juice and then saw the fried cheese. Emot had made saganaki and my mouth watered at the smell.

I coughed lightly and three sets of eyes swung my way and three chairs scraped the floor as they stood. Kai had to grab the back of his to keep it from toppling over. I walked closer and noticed the rest of the food was Greek as well, and I swear, I started drooling.

Emot stepped aside and held out his hand. "Care to join usss?" I nodded, and he slid the seat in for me before walking around the table to sit. Sic and Kai shared a look as they sat, and Kai handed me a glass of wine.

"You know I'm not twenty-one yet," was all I said, and they all began to laugh.

"Honey, this is Lasina, no cars, and no legal drinking age, most kids are drinking by fifteen here. Royalty has its advantages in this case, as well," Sic said, as he poured another glass for Emot. I watched Emot place pita points and taramasalata, caviar, bread, and potatoes mix on a plate. The pink paste is one of my all-time favorite dishes, along with skordalia, a garlic lemon potato paste, much like hummus. He also added some fried saganaki and zucchini chips, and then placed the plate directly in front of me.

To say I was ladylike in my eating of this would be an utter fallacy. I pigged the fuck out and didn't care who was watching me. The food was so fresh and so amazing that I could swear I was crying tears of joy. It didn't help that I hadn't really eaten since dinner the night before. After polishing off my plate, Emot handed me seconds and I worked my way through it more slowly.

The guys talked here and there, but I ignored the chatter in favor of the delicious food. The kitchen suddenly became silent, and a soft hissing could be heard off to my side. I looked down to see a tan and red saw scaled viper. I screamed at the top of my lungs and jumped onto the table knocking wine glasses over in the process.

A basilisk is one thing, a real snake is quite a bit different. The viper rubbed its scales together, to produce an eerie sound, similar to rubbing sandpaper together. It reared up as if to strike but began to transform into a small red-haired woman, with golden tanned skin. "I was told that the kings had a job for me." Emot helped me off the table, as Kai cleaned up the mess I made.

"How, in the fuck, can you change into a snake and not a basilisk?" I blurted out, still in shock at this tiny woman standing in front of me. Her black leather outfit was skin-tight, with more weapons than I could name attached to all sorts of places.

Her laughter was cynical at best, downright menacing at worst, but she answered my question nonetheless. "I'm only half basilisk, half-human. I can't fully shift into what you can, but I can shift into any snake I want. The saw scaled viper is the deadliest in the Earthly realm and the rarest here, the venom helps with my job. I'm an assassin. I typically pick nonvenomous snakes while doing recon work. Why have I been summoned?" Her last question was directed at Sic instead of me.

"We need you to gather intel on someone. He has been missing for some time and may require rescue. The only thing we know is that he is deep within the North Kingdom. He could be imprisoned, or he could be working for the king, we are unsure of his loyalties at this point. He is one of the Queen's mates, so please tread with caution on this one. We need to know if he is in league with the King or if he is being held prisoner, and how to best get him out if he is the latter. Time is not something we have a lot of so be swift," Sic laid it all out there, and she contemplated her next move while we watched in silence.

"I'll do it, on one condition. I want a night with her." She pointed in my direction and the guys all began to bristle.

"Absolutely not," Sic said without hesitation.

"Then you have my answer." She turned and began walking towards the stairs.

"Wait," I called, and she stopped in her tracks. "What kind of night are you asking for?"

She turned and smiled a devilish smile. "I think you know exactly what kind of night... I'll even let the kings watch. To say I've slept with the Queen would be worth dying for, and you're asking for an awful lot with this job."

I pondered her for a moment. She wasn't much older than I was. Red hair cascaded down to her hips, framing her full breasts. Her body was slim and small, lean where my own was curvy. "One night and they watch or stand guard, and no snake form. Take it or leave it."

"Done. I'll just be on my way North then; I'll be in *touch* very soon." I watched her sway her hips, as she walked up the

stairs and out of sight. Just as she rounded the corner the guys all exploded.

"Absolutely not."

"Are you joking?"

"You can't do that." I held up my hand and they stopped.

"You three have no say in the matter. Frankly, it's me she wants, it's my decision. If you need to find him so bad, then so be it. Besides, sleeping with her won't affect me losing my shift or not." I walked back around to my seat and began cleaning my plate up to wash it. A kitchen helper came to take it from me before I could even get two steps away from the table. I huffed, as she carried my plate to the sink and began cleaning.

I decided I had had enough of this shit, and walked out of the kitchen without another word. They could stew for all I cared, I still fully planned on making it home and never mating with a basilisk.

10

Maisie

I showered swiftly and found my favorite PJ shirt in a drawer. Sliding the cool cloth over my skin felt wonderfully comforting after the last few days. I walked out of the closet to see all three guys lined up by their doors. Then noticed the fourth door that remained closed at the end of the room.

I guess they had planned on having the Duke here by the time I got here, but circumstances proved otherwise. I ignored the three men standing by the side of the room and walked over to the window. I had almost gotten a chance to run today, maybe if I waited a bit before truly trying anything, they might relax their guard.

Once I was seated in the window seat, I heard them rustling a bit before I heard three doors close softly. Why had they waited? I didn't know and didn't care, I just wanted to go home. Even the stars look different here, their light a soft yellow against the purple-black backdrop of the sky. The night was so dark here that each star shone brighter than back home as well.

I don't know how long I sat but it felt like hours and yet only minutes. I heard the soft click of a door and then Kai sat across from me on the window seat. "Penny for your thoughts?" he whispered.

"Too many for just one penny.," I replied sarcastically.

"Then a quarter?" he bargained.

"I want to go home." I sighed and turned to look at him. "I never wanted this. Back home I had a life, friends, a boyfriend. Well, ex-boyfriend. I was going to get married and never mate with a basilisk, just so I could lose my shift." I looked back out the window at that last confession.

"Why would you want to lose your shift? Honestly, you would never lose it even if you weren't mated by twenty-one. It's an old wives' tale to make their children mate young and create babies." His words had the ring of truth, but I didn't want to believe them.

"How do you know that it isn't true? It could be, but everyone here is brainwashed to marry before then." I was getting defensive, not my greatest quality.

"I know it's true for several reasons. My cousin is the highest on the list, she just turned thirty and is still unmated. She can also still shift." My heart sank at his words. "Emot's mother, and yours for that matter, were both past twenty-one when they mated, and they never lost their shifts." With each new example, my heart sank lower.

"So, then it doesn't really matter, if I stay unmated, I'll always be this monster." My words were more to myself then to Kai, but he heard them all the same.

"I remember a little girl who loved the monsters. She used to ask about them every night. What happened to her, I wonder?" His words brought back memories of when I used to ask for stories about Lasina, before I knew what betrayal felt like.

"That girl died a long time ago. Now you have me." My words were harsh, more directed at myself than him.

"Maybe she isn't dead, but just hidden deep down inssside," his hiss became more pronounced as he said this. I turned to watch him slowly shift on the window seat, his body spilling onto the floor.

Even after all these years of denying my own monster within, his basilisk called to me. He was chalk white with red and blue diamonds running down his belly and back. His scales sparkled softly in the moonlight coming through the window. His head was almost as large as I was, with two straight blunt horns and a soft feather-like fan around them. He flicked his forked tongue out and then sighed.

"You sssmell like heaven," his words were a soft hiss, and then his tongue flicked along the base of my neck. "Sssee, ssshe callsss to me." I could feel my own basilisk begging to be set free, but I held her in check. I wouldn't shift again.

He backed away when he realized I wouldn't shift for him and curled around himself. "Why do you call her a monsssster?" he asked, once settled.

"Because she killed someone I loved dearly." Okay, so someone might be going a bit far, something I loved would be the truth. She killed the dog we had when I was fifteen, it had been an accident, but ever since then, I had kept her locked away.

"Ahh, yesss, I remember. Ssshe hurt your dog, but you know it was an accident, besssidesss, ssshe isss you and you are her. Ssso you are only punishing yourssself." I didn't want to remember that day so I turned away, but I could see him reflected perfectly in the glass. I could feel my basilisk begging to be released but I just held tighter onto the reins.

Kai flicked his tail out and wrapped it around my calf softly. I froze as it wound around my leg; the scales so soft that they felt like cool silk sliding on my skin. His eyes sparkled in the moonlight as he stroked behind my knee. I pushed his tail off my leg and curled it under my lap to keep him from doing it again. Instead of being deterred, he just laughed. "Oh, come now. Ssshow me your basilisk, pleassse."

He begged me sweetly, but I didn't want to shift. I could hear her keening for his altered form, and I knew that this night would end in a bed somewhere if I let her out, and frankly, I didn't want that, well, maybe only a tiny bit. "I think it's time for bed," I said, as I stood.

"Great idea." He wrapped his tail around my waist and lifted me off the floor.

I screamed as he carried me towards the bed. "Put me down." Two more doors flung open as Sic and Emot raced into the room just as Kai tossed me into the middle of the giant bed. His body taking up only a quarter of the space.

He used his tail to pull the covers over me and then his tongue licked a path from my shoulder to my ear. "Sssweet dreamsss, sssugar." I shivered at the contact, but hid it by pulling the covers up higher. Kai slid off the bed and shifted back into human form just as he reached his door. He winked once at me, then closed it softly behind him. Sic and Emot exchanged looks then walked back into their own rooms, leaving me blessedly alone.

11

Maisie

I woke to the sunlight streaming through the window and the smell of coffee wafting through the air. I didn't drink the stuff, but Mom always drank it in the mornings. I sat up and stretched opening my eyes. I expected to see my own room, but I was in the dead center of the massive bed. Damn, it had only been a dream. Sic walked through the main doors quietly with a steaming mug and froze when he saw me.

His mouth gaped open like I had two heads. "Um honey, do you realize you're naked right now?" I looked down my body and gasped, swiftly pulling the covers up to my chest. Tattered remains of my favorite shirt were scattered around the bed.

Sic walked closer with the coffee mug. "Would you like some coffee, or hot chocolate?" he asked, while trying not to stare at my nipples poking through the sheets.

"Hot chocolate would be great. Thank you." I looked down to ensure he couldn't see anything, and he set the mug on a side table.

"I'll let you get dressed, and for the record, we've all seen you naked from time to time, we don't exactly object." He turned and walked back out the doors, and closed them. I swiftly hopped

out of bed and raced to the safety of the closet to throw on a pair of pants and a t-shirt. I didn't feel like rummaging through the underwear again.

Once dressed, I walked back out to the room and grabbed the mug Sic had left, inhaling deeply. He had known I would choose hot chocolate from the beginning. I took a sip and sighed as the chocolate flavor burst on my tongue. I carried my cup as I walked through the main doors and into the living area. Emot had a table set up brunch style with an omelet station off to one side.

"Care for an omelet, love?" he asked, as he plated one for Sic.

I walked over and looked over the toppings but didn't see any broccoli. He must have read my mind because he bent down and pulled a small bowl of broccoli florets from under the table. He smiled knowingly, as he said, "If I don't hide them Kai will eat them all raw." He chuckled and began making me an omelet just the way I liked. Broccoli, cheese, and just a sprinkling of ham.

"Thank you," I said as he began to heap more cheese on top. Just like my mom used to do. If I didn't know any better, I would say she had told him.

"Once in a great while, your mom would bring us breakfassst. Usually, on daysss you had to get up sssuper early. She alwaysss made omeletsss, so I thought this might help you feel more at home here." He plated my food and handed it over, then started his own. Kai slid a chair out for me and then stole the bowl of broccoli from the omelet station, as Emot yelled at him to go away. Kai placed the bowl down in front of his plate and began popping broccoli onto every bite he took.

"Sasha mentioned that you met with the Nymphs yesterday at the lake," Sic spoke, while Emot pulled up a chair.

"Yes, the King offered me his son as a consort. I declined, of course, but invited him for dinner as a peace offering." I put another bite in my mouth and chewed as slowly as possible, so I didn't have to add more.

"You invited the Nymph King here for a meal? You do realize what that means, right?" Sic asked, shocked.

"They are so small, I figured they won't eat much, but then the guard told me that they can change to full size and I realized I might have been a bit too hasty. The damage is done now, besides how many people could he bring?" I continued to eat, as all three gaped at me.

Emot cleared his throat. "Well, let'sss sssay it's just the royal family that joins usss, we are looking at three thousand. I don't think we can accommodate that many, if they are full sssized, the nest just isssn't big enough."

I choked on a bite and coughed. "Did you say three thousand?"

Kai slapped my back and smiled. "Yes sugar, he did. The King has a thousand wives and consorts, they have almost fifteen hundred children and the heir himself has five hundred wives and consorts." It was my turn to gape.

"Oh," was all my brain could muster at the moment. "Maybe we ask just the King and his Queen to come, with the son and his main wife. Or we could ask them to remain small. Then we would have plenty of room." I was grasping at any idea that might smooth over my mistake.

"We can't just ask the King and Queen but, if we explain the situation they might agree to remain in their true form," Sic explained and rose from the table. "I'll go speak to His Majesty

now and sort out the details. Once we figure out a number we can better prepare for the meal. Emot go inform the chefs about the dinner and begin planning dishes we know that won't offend the Nymphs. Remember they are primarily vegetarian with only fish thrown in occasionally. Kai, you go prep the guards for any additional precautions that need to be taken with their arrival," Sic barked orders like a general, and they all began to fall in line to walk out.

"What about me?" I called, as Sic got to the door.

"Honey, you don't need to worry about a thing, we will take care of this." Kai and Emot waved but kept going on their assignments. "It is our job to see your wishes fulfilled, even if we must die to do so. That is what a mate does."

His words were soft, but I was even more troubled. "But we aren't mates Sic. You know that, right?"

He walked back over and knelt beside me. Cupping my cheek in his hand he placed his forehead to mine. "I pledged myself to you when you were eight years old. We have watched over you as mates are required to do. We built you a nest fit for the Queen of all Lasina, as mates are supposed to do. In my mind, you are my mate, consummated or not. Nothing will change that. The same goes for Kai and Emot, and if Zugo is still on our side he will feel the same." He kissed me softly on the cheek and then stood. "No matter how long it takes, you're our mate."

I watched him walk out the doors and all I could think to say after he left was a whispered, "But I'm not your mate."

12

Kai

I walked to the barracks, my home away from home. I was a soldier through and through. I took a deep breath of sweat and leather and sighed. "General Thuzo, might I have a moment?" I said, as I entered the General's quarters.

"Your Majesty, what may I do for you today?" He stood and shook my hand. Before I signed my name to the Treaty, I stood where Thuzo now stood, and was happy when he took my place. He was the perfect man for the job, and he was the perfect General.

"I need to inform you that we will be visited soon by the Nymphs. Queen Margaret has invited the King to dine, we are unsure at the moment how many will be joining us for this event, but I need you to make all necessary preparations for the Queen's safety. I will know more details when Sic returns from speaking to them. You will, of course, be given every able soldier should you need them, as long as Her Majesty is kept safe," I made my words brisk and to the point, most military men wanted it neat and tidy minus the bow.

"Yes, Your Majesty, I will place my best men nearest the Queen for any potential immediate danger and then add extra soldiers to the patrol on the evening of. We can also increase all security measures as more information arises." He detailed a few things and then began going over files of his soldiers like he wanted my opinion.

"I trust your judgment Thuzo. I will bring you the count when it is known, also whether they intend to be nymph-size or human-size. I'll let you get back to work." I turned to go when he stopped me with a hand.

"Before you leave, I have a personal matter I would like to discuss with you." He seemed hesitant. "Know that I have no desire to leave my post, but I have met someone from Saxdale, I wish to ask her to mate. She knows I live here, and that I don't want to retire yet, and she suggested I ask permission from Your Majesties before taking her as mate, since that would mean she would be moving here. She has no other mates and works as a seamstress there. I know that with Her Majesty now in residence her skills may come of value," he stopped the ramblings leaving his mouth.

"I am glad you have found someone that makes you happy. Yes, you may bring her here and mate with her. However, please don't let it cause any issues with your duties. You're the best General we've had." I smiled at his huge grin, and he shook my hand profusely.

"Thank you, thank you, thank you, Your Majesty." He ran his hand through his hair like a huge weight had been lifted.

"Go, the preparations can wait until all of the intel has come in. Go get your mate." He shook my hand again, and with a huge smile practically ran from the room.

I followed slowly, walking back out of the barracks. I walked towards the steward's office to relay the news. His office was on the ground level with a door to the courtyard. I knocked

and opened the door. The slim man was writing in some huge tome as I opened his door. His mate was making tea in their small kitchen. Yaga was as old as dirt and had chosen to live here from the day his office was complete. Ahxezo, his mate, joined him as soon as his kitchen had been complete. I had known Yaga's mate, Ahxezo, for many years and he was a wonder with sweets. I thought to have him make something special for Maisie.

"Kai my boy, have you come for my fresh cookies?" Ahxezo asked as he noticed me standing there.

"Unfortunately, no, I need to have a word with Yaga about something." I walked deeper into the room and he held a plate out just to tempt me. I grabbed a cookie before walking over to Yaga.

"I hope it's nothing serious," he replied to my back, as I stood before the desk.

Yaga looked up and startled, his hearing was going so he generally didn't hear me arrive. "Your Majesty, when did you arrive?" he half yelled.

I raised my voice slightly, so he could hear me better, "Just now, I need to talk to you about a mating. General Thuzo is hoping to bring a mate here. I wanted to make sure we had a home available for them." He smiled brightly at my words.

Ahxezo walked over and placed a hand on Yaga's shoulder smiling at my news. "Well, this is wonderful news, and yes, we have homes for those who choose to mate. Most have been waiting for Her Majesty to arrive. Now that she is here, I suspect the population of this castle will grow," Yaga yelled again. He also laughed and slapped his thigh at his last comment about the population growth.

I smiled and nodded, but Ahxezo noticed it didn't reach my eyes. "We will let you get back to work. I'll bring you your tea soon." He kissed Yaga on his balding head and then pulled me toward the kitchen. "Sit boy."

"I really don't have time for tea Ahx. I need to prepare for the Nymphs' arrival." He ignored my words and placed a hot cup of tea in front of my seat with two more cookies. He knew I would stay if there was food involved. I picked at the cookies while the tea cooled to a drinkable level.

"Spill it, boy, what's eating you?" he jumped straight to the point.

"Fuck, really. Are you fucking physic?" I asked deflecting.

He slapped my shoulder. "What have I told you about swearing in my kitchen, don't make me get the paddle, boy."

"Yes, sir. It's just Maisie. She wants to go home. I don't think she wants to mate with us, and I suspect she doesn't intend to stay long," I spilled swiftly.

He sat down across from me. "Give her time boy, she's just had her entire world turned upside down. Instead of focusing on mating her, take the time to get to know her, let her get to know you. Not in bed either." He patted my hand with his own wrinkled one. "Your mother would be so proud of you, boy. Make her proud now, and give Her Majesty time to get to know this world, you and the others, and herself. I suspect she has been hiding her true self for a very long time." He sipped his tea and sighed.

I chugged mine, only slightly burning my tongue, before eating my cookies. "Same old Kai, always in a hurry for the sweets. Why don't you take her some cookies?" He offered me a plate covered in cloth and then shooed me out of the house. He

waved from the front door. "We will make sure Thuzo and his mate have a wonderful house close to the castle."

I walked back into the castle to see chaos, as the kitchen staff ran around the great hall. Tables were being set up in tidy rows with long white clothes spread across the tops. I carried the plate of cookies up the stairs and into our room. Maisie was sitting in the window seat.

"I brought cookies," I called out. She looked up and smiled, as I sat the plate in front of her and pulled the cloth off. "Hot and fresh from Ahxezo. He's the steward's mate." I sat next to her and looked out the window.

13

Maisie

Kai sat next to me and watched the Gryphons. I had been mesmerized by them for most of the day. "They are doing a mating dance. Trying to attract the females that stay in the tree line." He pointed towards a small stand of trees close to the base of the mountain. "The males do aerial dances and also battle to be the first chosen to breed."

"So those are only males? Why don't the females join them?" I was curious, Gryphons were nothing more than mythical creatures on the Earthly realm but they were real.

"Right now, yes, it's just the males. The females will join them as the sun begins to set, and then they begin to pair off. The females will choose their male and they will mate," he was explaining their mating rituals but wasn't seeing the problem I was having. I didn't get to choose my mates. These Gryphons were freer than I would ever be.

I grabbed a cookie that was warm and gooey and began to eat. The flavor reminded me of home and Mom, and Feeling the tears begin to gather, I refused to cry over this or anything. I was strong, I would get home to Mom. I vowed it.

Kai reached out and wiped his thumb along my lower lip. "You had chocolate on your face," was all he said. I felt tingles travel across the skin he touched, and a low hiss in my ear as my basilisk awoke. She wanted him for a mate, but I refused to let her out.

I turned away from his face and returned my attention to the Gryphons as I finished the last two cookies on the plate. "You know, you do still have a choice. I have five brothers, Emot has three, and Sic, fuck, he has about a dozen. Although the youngest is five. As far as the Duke is concerned, well any one of the higher-class men in the North could replace him," his words were soft, and I could hear the sadness as he spoke. It was as if he didn't want me to choose someone else.

"It isn't you guys that's the issue. I had no say, how is that fair to me? Did anyone take into consideration how I may feel about this?" I spat out. I could hear the bitterness in my tone.

"I know it isn't what you would have chosen, but I still remember a little girl who was happy about marrying Princes. Have you really killed off all that the little girl wanted?" he was still speaking softly, as if we were in a room full of people and he wanted no one else to hear.

"That little girl grew up," I simply said.

"But did she really go away? Admit that your basilisk is begging to be out. That's why every night you've shifted in your sleep." I looked at him in shock.

"That's not true. I didn't shift last night," I could hear the defensiveness in my tone.

"Yes, you did sugar. Gods, she is beautiful. Scarlet red with just a hint of pale pink on your underbelly, green swirls along

your spine," his voice had gone all wistful, like he desperately wanted to see it again. "Don't get me wrong, this form is more than pleasing, but she calls to us all. Your basilisk is one of a kind, sugar, and the world would do anything for you."

"How do you know I shifted? You've seen my form many times over the years, I'm sure." He smirked at my words.

"We know you shifted because it forces our shifts. Your basilisk calls to ours, so when she is out, ours come charging forward." He looked over at me and smiled.

"Oh, I didn't realize that happened. Why does it happen though?" I was curious now.

"Because our basilisks are mates, regardless of what we want as people, our basilisks have been mates since those signatures went on paper. Our basilisks are an extension of us. We wouldn't have signed without them being fully aware of the implications. Your mother told you about us so much when you were young, your basilisk thinks of us as her mates. Even without the consummation, she calls them to her," he explained, and deep down I could tell he was right; my basilisk hissed her confirmation that they were hers.

"Why was I never told about the Duke then?" It was the one thing that didn't add up.

"Because your mother didn't know about the Duke until after he had been added. She's never met him, never seen him, and therefore couldn't tell you about him. She's known us since we were children. The Duke's family was reclusive even before your mother left. She wouldn't have met him as a child." I listened to his words but couldn't tell if he was truthful or not, I guessed it would just have to wait until I met him.

Kai scooted closer and leaned in towards my face. His hand cupped my cheek and my basilisk purred, if that's even the word for the utterly pleased sound she made. He slid his thumb along my jaw before tilting my head up to look at his. "I don't care how long I have to wait. I won't leave you, and my basilisk won't leave yours." He pulled me to his chest and planted his mouth softly to mine. He didn't demand just lingered with his lips pressed gently to mine.

Just then the door opened, and he pulled back. I couldn't control the blush that tinted my skin as Sic and Emot walked into the room. "I have news," Sic called, as Emot looked between Kai and me.

Kai cleared his throat and Emot hid a smile. "What news? Did your meeting with the Nymph King go well?"

"The King understands our special restrictions and has asked if we would be agreeable to having just his son, himself, and five wives each. I told him that would be more than acceptable, and they will be joining us tomorrow night for dinner at sundown." Sic smiled at this news since it meant that the castle wouldn't be overrun with Nymphs.

Kai stood and glanced at me one last time before picking up the plate. "I'll go let Thuzo know the numbers. If he is back yet... Oh, I almost forgot, he has found a mate and is bringing her back to the castle. She is a seamstress if we ever have a need for one." He walked towards the door, glancing over his shoulder one last time before closing it behind him.

14

Maisie

Emot looked at me questioningly as he sat down in Kai's vacated seat. I tried to ignore his gaze while Sic continued talking. Once Sic had laid out all the details, which I really didn't listen to, he looked at me. "You have a bit of chocolate right here." He pointed to his own face and I hastily licked my lips clean. Sic watched my tongue dart out with a hungry stare, before walking back to the door. "I'm going to make sure we have all the preparations in order."

Emot and I both laughed as Sic walked towards the door, adjusting himself on the sly. Once Emot saw the door close, he turned to me and said, "Ok, ssspill it. Did I really ssee you and Kai lip locking?"

I blushed again and looked out the window. "He kissed me, if you must know."

"Ssso. Did you like it?" he continued, scooting closer to me on the window seat. "I promissse I won't tell a sssoul."

"Why are you so interested if I liked it or not, it was one stupid kiss?" I sounded defensive, even to my own ears.

"Kai isss different than Sssic and me. There are waysss for malesss to be together obviousssly, and Sssic and me, we actually enjoy it. Kai only ever... how do I put this nicely... joined in, on the very rare occasssion when you and Sssam got rowdy. Mossst of the time he would jussst take care of himsssself, but thossse nightsss, well they got to usss all," his words where not unkind, just a statement of fact, but I still felt bad. Probably because they had to wait for ten years and I just did whatever I wanted during that time. "He alssso never let either of usss do things to him."

"Since you're being so forthcoming with the information, why did you and Sic sign if you're both into guys?" He laughed at my question.

"It would be easssier to say in human termssss, Sic and I are bi. Kai is sssstraight. The Duke, well I have no clue, ssso let's just say sssstraight. We actually didn't begin any relationsssship until a few years after we signed. We did the typical guysss night out and got wasssted, trying to pick up chicksss that totally ssshot us down and he and I ended up in bed together later that night. I'm guesssssing this isssn't newsss to you though?" He looked at me as if waiting for an answer.

"Not entirely, no. Kai explained the various ways basilisks can have... sex." I blushed; it was one thing to have sex, but another to talk so openly about it. Hell, my mother had stumbled her way through the birds and bees talk, and she had only explained the human version. "But do you want only him?" I had to know; my curiosity was my worst enemy.

"I love Sssic, but he isssn't why I signed that Treaty. Originally, we all sssigned it to bring peace and reunify Lasina. However, over the yearsss, watching you grow up from a sssscrawny kid, to this beautiful young woman hasss made usss all develop a desssire for you as a person. That'ssss why we all

stayed; we could've backed out at any point," his words were softer than I expected.

"I honestly don't know how I feel about this whole situation. I want to go home, but a part of me wants to stay. I just feel like I was cheated out of my choice in this matter." I looked away from Emot and continued watching the Gryphons, the females had just joined the males in the sky, and they slowly began to pair off.

Emot leaned his back against the window just inside my field of vision. "You are the one piece of the Treaty that is ssset in sssstone. You are the Queen, no one elssse. I know Kai told you all of us are replaceable and he'sss right. I won't lie though; we would all be disssappointed if you choossse sssomeone other than ussss." Emot stood and looked down at me. "I guessss my reasssoning for wanting to know if you liked it, wasss to see if we had any ssshot at all," with that said, he left.

I watched him walk out the main doors leaving me with nothing but my thoughts and the sound of the fire that seemed to always crackle in the large fireplace. I turned back to the window and watched the sun begin to lower over the lake. My thoughts turned to Kai and his kiss. My lips tingled as I thought of his mouth pressed against mine, and my basilisk hissed in appreciation. I felt my skin begin to crawl and saw scales begin to rise up, just under my skin. She wanted out, but I didn't want her anymore. At this, her hiss turned nasty and she pressed harder trying to escape. I held back the shift barely, before she subsided.

I climbed to my feet as the dying sun sank below the horizon and walked to go find something to eat. Time seemed to be similar to Earth, but I haven't seen a clock to know for sure. Once I rounded the bottom of the stairs, I ran into a young woman looking on in awe as the servants rushed around with all sorts of decor. "Oh, I'm so sorry," I said as she turned.

"Your Majesty." Her eyes widened and she sank deep into a curtsy. "I am so sorry."

"It was my fault I wasn't paying attention to where I was going." I tried to get her to rise but she stayed low to the ground.

"Sage, there you are," I heard a male voice call out, and then a large man appeared around the corner. "Your Majesty," he spoke, before bowing low.

"You must be General Thuzo," I asked, noticing his military uniform covered in metals of high rank.

"Yes, Your Majesty, and this is my soon-to-be mate, Sage." He gestured to the woman who was still bowed low.

"Please stand Sage, it was entirely my fault. I should have paid better attention to where I was going." I watched Sage slowly rise and a blush spread across her face as she looked at Thuzo. "Congratulations to you both. If you will excuse me, I'm in search of dinner." They both bowed again as I began walking towards the kitchen.

I walked down into the kitchen again and it was chaos, people were rushing everywhere and Emot was giving orders like a general himself. I paused in the doorway, so I was out of the way, and watched. Emot's forehead was covered in sweat and he had his sleeves rolled up showing off his toned biceps. I felt my basilisk purr her pleasure at the sight of his prowess.

I heard the sound of footsteps and backed into the darkness of the stairwell to keep from being caught staring. "He is a magnificent sight, is he not?" the question whispered into my ear had my heart jumping into my throat. I spun around only to be pinned to Sic's hard chest as he backed me to the wall.

My basilisk preened at his nearness and it took everything in me not to shift on the spot. His bare chest was covered with scales as if he was having trouble keeping his own in check. His head dipped to my neck and I felt his lips trail up to my earlobe softly. "He'ss magnificent to watch. You sshould ssee other thingss he'sss magnificent at." His hiss was becoming more prevalent as more scales bloomed on his arms. He stepped back and let his shift fully take over before flicking his tongue out just a bit to smell the air. "I can tassste the desssire coming from you," with that, he turned and left me standing alone in the stairwell.

"Do you think Viper will find Zugo?" I couldn't help asking, as Emot sat back down at the small kitchen table. Sicrin had told him I was hiding in the stairwell and now the three of us were seated at the small table in the kitchen. Occasionally, Emot would get up to direct the staff, but he always came back when he was done. Sic sat shirtless picking at his plate while I devoured everything Emot put in front of me to try.

"I think she's our best shot at locating him," Sic said throwing his napkin down. "I'm done, I'll see you upstairs in thirty, right Emot?"

I watched as Emot blushed. "Yeah, I'll be up sssoon."

Sic walked off and I couldn't help but glance at Emot's red face. "What was that all about?"

"Kai asssked for a favor, to keep him from doing sssomething sssstupid. It's not sssomething we haven't done before, but well you're here now, sssso it'sss a bit awkward." His face got even redder as he spoke.

"I'm guessing that Kai asked for something sexual, and you don't want to tell me about it because you think I would be

upset?" I had to admit even to myself that I was entirely too curious about them having sex, and a bit turned on. I could feel my basilisk aching to be let out at the idea of seeing them all together.

"Would that upsssset you?" he asked quietly, as if not really wanting to hear my answer.

"I don't have a problem with you having sex with Sic. So, why would I have an issue with you having sex with Kai?" I replied.

"Well, he didn't exactly ask to have ssssex. The only thing he ever asksss for is a blow job. I think the only reassson he even doesss that issss because women won't touch us." He didn't say it, but I knew it was because of me that women wouldn't touch them.

I began to feel guilty about everything these three had given up just for the sake of peace in the Kingdoms. Did I really have the right to run away when they had sacrificed so much? Not counting Zugo, and the possibility that he may have given up his freedom entirely to sign that Treaty.

"You can go. I'll be up later. I'm going to walk outside in the courtyard." I stood and Emot stood with me. He didn't say anything, but I knew he was watching me as I walked away. I rounded the stairs until I reached the main hall; the guards opened the door to the courtyard as I approached. I wasn't used to all the pomp and ceremony around this place and it was beginning to grate on my nerves.

The night air was cool against my face, and I couldn't help the sigh of relief at being alone. My thoughts raced in all directions. The kiss I shared with Kai. Being thrown into the Kingdom I really knew nothing about, and was expected to rule. The Treaty that signed my life away to four men I had never met.

My mother's fate; was she alive or dead? My father; was he still in the Earthly realm or had he somehow made it back? Zugo; if he even still existed and if Viper could find him. Emot and Sic; everything about them had me questioning my life.

I was walking along the parapet wall as my mind turned over all these things. And then there was Sam. I realized I was crying when I reached the corner of the outer wall and the landscape before me was blurry.

I heard a soft giggle off to my right and swiped away tears just as General Thuzo and Sage rounded the corner. "Oh, Your Majesty, so sorry to disturb you," Thuzo's voice was soft, as he tried to pull Sage back around the corner. Sage stopped him and whispered something and then he nodded and walked off.

"Your Majesty? Is everything alright?" Sage asked, as she stepped closer. Maybe if I had someone to talk to, I would feel better. Before I knew what came over me, I was spilling everything that had happened in the last several days, even going so far as to tell her about Sam, the guys. I didn't mean to spill it all, it just tumbled out, and by the time I was finished, I was bawling again.

Sage hugged me close and rubbed my back while I cried it out on her shoulder. "No wonder you're so distracted. I would be too if my life had been upended like that. But I can tell you, Kai, Sicrin, and Emot are good men. They love their Kingdoms and have helped so many in need, without ever being asked." She circled her hand over my shoulders the way a mother would to her own child. "My humble opinion, for what it's worth. I think you should give them a chance, at least get to know them before you make any decisions about going back. I also know that if your mother is still alive, she would tell you the same thing. If she is alive, I can feel that she is trying to get back to you." My tears had stopped, and I realized she was a voice of reason I had needed.

"Thank you, Sage and I'm sorry for ruining your date night." I smiled and wiped the last of the tears away.

"Thuzo and I have many years ahead of us, with date nights aplenty. You are our Queen, and we both want to see you happy. All of Lasina wants you to be happy, because it means that we have finally achieved unity." She smiled at me and then asked, "Do you want me to walk with you back inside?"

I shook my head no and said. "I'm going to stay here a bit longer. You go be with Thuzo, and thank you, Sage."

"Have a wonderful night, Your Majesty." She remarked before walking off towards the lower courtyard. I watched as Thuzo embraced her when she reached him, and then they walked towards the outbuildings.

I looked up at the deep purple sky and took a deep breath. I would do as she suggested and try to get to know the guys and Lasina. My mother would have wanted that, and if she was dead, I would honor her memory this way, at least.

16

Zugo

The sound of dripping water was all I could hear in the pitch-black darkness. No light permeated the dungeon as I slumped against the wall in my chains. Chains that had kept my basilisk locked away for ten whole years. The day after I signed the Treaty, Vago had my family killed and I was placed into this cell. I knew deep down he couldn't kill me, or the terms of the Treaty would allow another to take my place, but after years in captivity, I had lost all hope of freedom.

I sat silently, contemplating the ways I could hurry my death along, when a new sound began to reach my ears. The sound of sandpaper grating against itself was deafening in the silence surrounding me. My dark adjusted eyes barely made out the snake slithering through the bars of my cell, and I welcomed the bite it could give.

Instead of the strike I hoped would come the snake transformed into a woman barely visible in the dark. "Are you Zugo, the Duke?" the woman standing before me whispered close to my face, as it hung limply against my chest.

"I used to be, but that was a very long time ago. Now I am just seeking death," I whispered back.

She began to reach for my wrists, and I began to hear metal scraping as she did something to the cuffs. After several moments, I heard a click and felt my wrist slide free of the metal that had bound it tight. She moved to the other side and began to repeat the process. Once I was free, my basilisk screamed to life and I shifted unwillingly in the too small of a space.

"Hey buddy, you're crushing me into the wall. Mind shifting back?" the small woman's voice sounded strained, as my basilisk began to slowly recede into my human form. She gasped for breath and grumbled about big snakes, before saying a grudging 'thanks'.

I turned swiftly and grabbed her by the throat, pinning her to the wall. "Who are you, and why are you here?"

She held up her arms in a gesture of peace, but I still didn't release her. I squeezed just enough to get her to speak and she hissed, "My name is Viper, the Queen sent me to find you. So, found you I did. Now I'm going to get you out of here and at least to a safe house until they can come rescue you." I stopped squeezing and dropped her to the floor, again my energy spent.

"What Queen? Clara?" I asked, as she adjusted her clothing and began walking towards the cell door. She began working a set of tools into the lock and focused on her task.

I heard the click of the lock and then she answered my question. "No, the Queen of Lasina sent me. Your mate, I believe." She swung the door open and looked around the hall. "It's clear, let's go."

She worked her way down the hall, making several turns until we reached an area with low light and I had to shield my eyes at the brightness. I saw half a dozen bodies around the floor as my eyes slowly began to adjust to the low light. She grabbed

my hand and pulled. "We don't have much time before the changing of the guards, and they find this mess. Let's go." She swung open another door and the smell of fresh air blasted my face.

We ran out into the night and I felt tears sting my eyes as the implications of my freedom fully hit home. She kept running until we hit the tree line and I dropped to the ground shifting to rub my scales against cool dirt and rough rock for the first time in ten years. "I'm free," I whispered into the dark, as I watched her shift into a saw scaled viper. She slithered farther into the forest and hissed. I followed her until we reached a stream with a little cottage tucked into the side of a hill.

Viper shifted swiftly and pounded on the door. It opened just a crack and an identical young woman whispered something I couldn't hear, before the door was swung wide and Viper looked at me to shift. I shifted back and walked into the one room cottage. The smell of fresh meat and food had my empty stomach aching.

The young woman placed a large bowl of stew down at the table and I attacked it the way a hellhound would attack a leprechaun. They continued to whisper as I shoveled food in as fast as possible, not even bothering to chew. Viper walked over and placed a hand on my shoulder. "You will be safe here until I can get a rescue team together. Try not to hurt my sister. Cobra will see that you have plenty of food and a place to sleep."

With those words, she walked back out the door and left me with this 'Cobra' woman. I heard a lock fall into place and then she slid into the seat across from me. "Would you like a bath? I can have one ready for you shortly." The idea of cleaning years of grime off my body sounded heavenly so I nodded while I continued to eat.

Cobra stood and walked into a room, I heard the sound of running water, and then she walked back out to the table. "Why don't you take a break on the food, so you don't get sick, and you can get washed up." She pulled the almost empty bowl away and pulled me to stand. She led me into the bathroom and helped me step into the tub. I hadn't even realized that my clothes had disintegrated years ago.

I sat in the steaming water and sighed as the heat worked its way into my bones. She sat on a stool and helped me wash my hair and back. It was the first real contact I had had with anything in ten long years, and I couldn't help the way my body reacted to her touch. My cocks hardened at the thought of feeling a woman for the first time, and I rushed to cover them, only to hear her soft laugh.

"I'm a prostitute Zugo, there is no need to cover what I see more frequently than you do." Her hands trailed over my chest and then were wrapping around the base of both my cocks. She squeezed them together and began stroking me. I couldn't hold back the groan as pleasure began to run away with my senses. Her soap-coated hands slid in a steady rhythm until I was gripping the side of the tub. I moaned as my release spread through me, relaxing me even more.

Cobra used water to rinse my cum off, and the soap that still coated my body, before helping me stand. "I won't have sex with you, if only because you're mated to the future Queen, but I will gladly help you in any way I can. Now, after you dry off, come sit by the fire and have some more stew. We need to get you back to full strength."

Maisie

Several days had passed since Viper left on her mission when she arrived back at the castle. I just walked in from the courtyard and was about to get ready for bed when I heard her distinctive slither. Chills raced up my spine as she entered the main rooms. She shifted in the main room before knocking on my door then walking through the opening. "I have found Zugo and helped him escape from the dungeons he was held captive in," she blurted as soon as she was through the door. "He is currently in a safe house with my sister."

My basilisk hissed at the thought of him with another woman, but I had never met him so why did I care? I pushed my basilisk down some and she began to talk some more. "He was being harnessed by magic cuffs that wouldn't allow him to shift or escape. He's very weak at the moment but should recover. My sister is an amazing healer, when she's not busy with a client."

Her words raced by me and I realized the guys needed to hear this. I ran to Kai's door, not bothering to knock, and opened it wide. Just as the door hit the wall, I saw Sic and Emot on their knees, each one bobbing on one of Kai's cocks. I had totally forgotten they were in there and the sight had me blushing, while my basilisk hummed her appreciation. I couldn't look away from both men as they worked in a rhythm of one on, one off. Kai's

hands were fisted into their hair and his head was thrown back. Viper stood next to me in the doorway. "Well now, I could watch this all night."

Kai's head pulled forward at Viper's words and his eyes locked with mine. His face a picture of ecstasy, as he groaned his release. I couldn't help but shift from side to side as I realized how turned on I was by watching them. Just rubbing my thighs together had my basilisk scales rising to the surface of my body. Viper hummed her own appreciation as Emot and Sic stood. Kai quickly tucked both his cocks away and then was walking toward the door.

He pulled me into the room and then shut the door in Viper's face. "I'm sorry Maisie, you shouldn't have had to see that. You also shouldn't be shamed in front of Viper like that. Can you forgive us?" He truly looked worried about my reaction.

Sic slid closer and flicked his snake tongue out. His eyes darkened before he spoke softly, "Can't you smell how wet she is Kai? Watching us turns her on. But that isn't why she interrupted, is it?"

I couldn't look away from Kai, worrying my lower lip, and trying to rein in my basilisk who was fighting for freedom with what she wanted as hers. "Viper found Zugo," was all my tongue-tied self could manage. Emot sped past us and opened the door again, walking into my bedroom.

"You found him, where, and how can we get him out?" Sic and Kai followed as Emot began throwing questions at Viper, and I just stood battling my basilisk back, so I didn't shift.

"Slow your roll, sonny. He's safe. I was able to break him out of the dungeon, and he is currently with my sister recovering. She lives out in the forest, and only she and I know where the

house is. He needs to gain some strength before we try to get him over the wall," she was brisk in her explanation, but the guys were still not satisfied.

"Can we send a healer to him? Someone we can trust." Sic asked, while Viper's gaze swung my way.

"I figure it will take a week for him to gain enough strength to be able to travel to the wall. It's only a two-hour hike from her house, but it's up the mountain on the far north side. Your rescue team will need to skirt the wall until you hit the sea, and then you will be close to where the meet up point needs to be." She ran through more details as the guys listened and her gaze swung to mine after answering all of their questions. "I believe, I've more than upheld my end of the bargain. Now for my payment," Her words softened, and she licked her lower lip.

"You want her to pay up now?" Kai asked, as she smiled.

"Most definitely. Call it motivation for me to want to continue to help your friend." She crooked her finger in my direction and I stepped forward some.

"I've never been with a woman before," I confessed, and the guys all swung their gazes my way. I blushed under their scrutiny.

"Don't worry, Your Majesty, all you need to do is lay back and enjoy." She circled behind me and whispered into my ear, "Maybe we should let the guys watch." She pushed me towards the bed, while the guys stood mesmerized. "Yes or No, Your Majesty?" I couldn't make a coherent sentence if I tried, so I just shook my head yes as if hypnotized.

She spun me around so I was facing the door, I couldn't help but blush as I realized the guys would be able to see

everything. I watched her movements closely as she grasped the hem of her shirt and pulled it up over her head, revealing her full breasts. She dropped her pants quickly, so she stood naked in front of me. Her lips descended on mine and my eyes slid shut to drown out everything but her.

Viper's hand slid down to my waist and slowly inched my shirt up until she had to break our kiss to remove it altogether. I felt her mouth return to my lips briefly, before she kissed her way to my neck and began a heated descent towards my collarbone. I felt her hands flick the button of my pants and then she was pushing them down taking my panties with them.

Her head dipped lower and I felt the heat of her breath on my nipple just before she sucked it into her mouth. I felt her tongue flick my nipple as she sucked, first one side and then the other. By the time I felt the cool air on my hardened peak, I was aching for more. I opened my eyes momentarily. "Climb up onto the bed but stay on your knees," was all she said, when I locked eyes with her.

I crawled slowly to the center of the bed and felt her slide up behind me. "Turn around Your Majesty." I turned and got a quick glance at the guys all groaning as they watched Viper touch my skin. "Should we make them give us a show while I make you scream in pleasure?" her question was rhetorical, as she barked orders, "You wanna watch, strip." I could feel my pussy flood at her command, and all three began shedding clothes like they couldn't do it fast enough.

She pulled my hand to her body and began to caress her own breasts with my fingers, while she trailed her other hand down towards my clit. I closed my eyes as her finger circled my clit once before trailing between my lips for the wetness there. Her nimble fingers worked their way between my folds briefly, then slid back to that bud of nerves, and she began in earnest. My

fingers continued to explore her body until I was mimicking her movements as my own hand slid down to her core.

Viper slapped my hand away and commanded, "Just feel, my Queen, let me worship you." She began to sink her mouth lower capturing my nipple between her teeth and I couldn't hold back my moan. She looked up my body and then whispered, "Watch them stroke themselves just for you." I couldn't help but look up at the guys and she had been right all three had cocks in hand, stroking away. "Just keep watching them, my Queen."

My eyes were glued to all three as I felt her tongue dip into my navel before continuing further still. I gasped out loud as her mouth descended onto my core and her fingers began to slide deep into my body. Her hum of appreciation vibrated through me and my body began to tighten as she drew me closer to orgasming.

I felt a tingle ripple across my legs and briefly glanced down to see that Viper has shifted into a very large python, her forked tongue still flicking my clit. Viper began to wind herself up my thigh and around my waist squeezing just enough to lift my breasts high. She draped herself over my shoulder to flick her tongue along my nipple just as I felt the tip of her tail enter my pussy. It felt so much better than I would have ever imagined a snake's tail to feel. Her body flexed and relaxed as she began using her tail to fuck me. The guys all groaned as they watched my snake dressed body and they pumped themselves in time with Viper.

She rolled her muscles along my clit sending shockwaves through my body as I got closer to sweet release. My basilisk purred her happiness and it came out of my mouth as a moan, and then I felt Viper curl her tail just a touch, and I broke. My screams of release had my eyes closing and my head falling back, while my body clamped around her tail. She continued to thrust harder and faster. The more I reacted the harder she fucked, until I was lost

to nothing but sensation. She brought me to orgasm after orgasm without even giving me a moment to breath. The guys finished rapid fire while she had me overwhelmed by sensation.

She slowly unwound before shifting back then I collapsed onto the bed. Viper slid up my body and kissed my lips one last time, tangling her tongue briefly with mine. I vaguely felt the bed dip as she slid off it, blissful sleep taking over.

I woke the next morning more relaxed until the realization that the guys saw everything, hit me full force. I pulled the covers over my head even though the guys were nowhere around. "Stupid, Maisie. Just stupid." I heard a door open and stopped talking to myself.

"Shh she is still asleep," I heard what sounded like Kai, as footsteps sounded in the room.

Sic's voice whispered to me even under the covers as he asked. "Do you think Viper found Zugo yet?" I almost bolted upright at his question. Viper had been here last night, and I remembered in vivid detail them watching us have sex. Hell, I watched them get off, while watching me.

Emot's soft hiss entered the conversation as they walked out the main doorway, "We will jussst have to wait and sssee." The door closed behind them softly and I unburied myself from the covers. What in the actual fuck?

I slid from the bed and walked to the bathroom to shower and dress, before opening the main doorway. Viper was standing in the doorway, seemingly filling in the guys for the first time when I approached. "He is weak and will need time to recover

before he can make it to the designated meeting place." The guys looked at me as Viper spoke, and then Sic remembered what her payment would be and his face darkened.

"I sssuppose you will want your payment now?" His hiss more evident as his anger rose.

Emot pulled him to the side of the room, and I could see he was trying to calm the situation down. Kai stood looking between me and Viper like he was imagining us in bed together. Viper just smiled and looked me dead in the eyes. "No payment is necessary boys, now I really must be off." She winked, and I realized she had done something to make them forget they had watched us.

Sic relaxed as she turned and walked away, and Kai's face turned downtrodden. "Damn, I wanted to watch the two of you." It took everything I had not to laugh at his face before he shrugged. "Who's hungry?" He walked out the door before looking back. Sic and Emot just rolled their eyes before following.

I watched them walk down the central stairway just as a tiny sand boa circled my foot. Slapping my hand over my mouth as I was about to scream, it slowly shifted, and Viper was standing in front of me. "Are you really scared of snakes?" She asked, as her eyes filled with laughter.

"I had one bite me when I was young, they aren't my favorite." She laughed at my explanation and then stepped closer until her breasts pressed mine.

"I made sure they didn't remember last night, just in case you might feel awkward." She slid her hand along my neck and pulled me close, pressing her lips to mine. "It was my pleasure to pleasure you, my Queen." Stepping back, she shifted once more to slither off, to wherever it was she was going.

I walked into the kitchen and found chaos in the form of fruits and veggies. There were carrots, potatoes, all sorts of green things, and fruit crates littering the kitchen. It looked like a grocery store produce section exploded in the kitchen. Emot was once again the general in charge of the masses as workers ran to and fro. Sic and Kai were sitting out of the way eating breakfast, an extra plate waiting with a covered lid.

I went to sit down in the same spot as yesterday, when Kai pulled the chair out from the spot with the dome. "Emot made you a plate before he went to work," he said, as I seated myself. The kitchen looked like a tornado had hit and Emot was directing everything like a conductor.

Cold dishes were being prepared and placed in the large walk-in fridge, as other prep work was going on for later. A large man in a chef's hat and coat was making all sorts of chocolate decorations that I was dying to try. Kai picked up the silver cover and the delicious smell of bacon hit my nose. I turned my attention to the food in front of me and shoveled it down as fast as possible. Kai walked over to Emot while I was eating and when he returned, he held a tiny chocolate rose.

"I'll make a deal with you," he paused waiting for my nod to continue, "I'll give you this one of a kind chocolate flower, if you spend an hour with me in the gardens." His smile told me he knew it was the worst sort of bribery.

It took less time than I expected for me to make the choice to go with him. "Ok, but only an hour." I placed that caveat on the deal and rose. Kai pulled my arm into his while simultaneously handing me the tiny flower. He wrapped his large hand over my smaller one as it rested in the crook of his elbow, then escorted me out of the kitchen.

We walked in silence up the stairs to the courtyard doors. The guard opened them for us and closed them once more after we passed through. Vermillion sunlight streamed over the walls, surrounding us, as we walked between the slim trees. Once a bench came into view, he guided me towards it and sat, pulling me into his lap. I shifted swiftly and pointed a finger in his face. "That wasn't a part of the deal."

Kai licked the tip of my finger laughing. "Yes, but it's much better than sitting on the cold hard concrete, at least I'm warm," he whispered, heavily implying that he was still hard. I wiggled slightly only to have his hand grasp my hip. He hissed through his teeth, "Pleassse don't."

I stopped instantly, standing to pace, my energy getting the better of me. "So, why did you want to spend the hour with me?" I asked, trying not to force anything, but if he wasn't going to talk I would. "I mean, you know everything there is to know about me. What more could you want to know?"

His laughter was rich and full, sending ripples of pleasure across my skin and straight down to my clit. "That might be true, but you know nothing of us. Since we are to be mated, don't you think you should get to know us?" his words made me stop and realize just how conceded my words sounded. I had made the decision to try the other night before Viper arrived.

"You're right, I'm sorry, I should make the effort to get to know you and the others." I felt like a selfish ass for my words. I sat next to him on the bench bouncing my leg nervously, not knowing what to say.

"Are you nervous?" he asked, placing a hand on my leg to still the movement.

"Kinda, I don't know. I just don't know what to ask. It seems mundane to ask you the inane questions like what your favorite color is, when we are basically married already." His thumb rubbed my leg as I spoke, gesturing wildly with my hands.

"Then don't ask those types of questions. What do you want to know, I will answer anything?" He was still rubbing my thigh and warm tingles were spreading from his touch.

"Do you like men?" I blurted, and then slapped my hands over my mouth.

His laughter was deeper and full-bellied, causing laugh lines to crinkle the corners of his eyes. I found myself drawn to them, wanting to touch them but kept my hands locked over my mouth. Wiping his eyes, he calmed down enough to look at me. He pulled my hands away from my mouth, smiling the whole time. "Is that what you most desperately want to know?"

I thought for a moment before speaking, "Emot mentioned that he and Sic were bi, and he did also say you were straight. But just last night, I saw you with them." Trying to explain was difficult without flat out saying that I had seen them blowing him.

He didn't seem upset that I had asked and that was a relief, so when his answer came, I was somewhat surprised. "I'm not bi, per se, but not straight either. How to put this delicately?" He paused and pondered his words for a moment before starting once again, "Since you were eight, the world has known we were yours. That also meant that any sort of carousing, we might have done, ended. At first, it wasn't a big deal with us still being teens, and frankly, even your hand works. As we got older needs began to grow, not just for sex, but comfort as well."

"Basilisks love heat and contact, even in human form. They began having a sexual relationship while I continued to deny

103

myself. One night I got utterly wasted, I think that was about the time you realized what masturbation was." I blushed at his words, but he just smiled and continued, "I came back to the nest just trashed and hard as a fucking rock. Sic and Emot were in bed together when I stumbled in and just watched."

He looked up to the lavender sky for a moment as if seeing that night all over again. "Sic saw me and then before I know it, he was letting me fuck him while he fucked Emot. I don't know exactly how it happened, but it did. I felt bad for intruding on their relationship. Eventually, we all sat down and discussed it, and while I won't take it from either, I do enjoy giving it to them, and occasionally getting blowjobs. So, while I'm not bi, I'm not quite straight either. Does that answer your question?" He looked me in the eye as he asked, and I nodded.

The way he spoke had my basilisk pressing on my skin as if she was pleased, and also, I could feel the need to be touched coming from her. I rose to get a bit of space between us before my basilisk made me do something stupid and I felt scales on my arms. Seeing his own white scales appear on his arms had me running, not in fear of him but of what I might do.

"Maisie, wait," he called as he followed me at a slower pace. Hitting the wall, I stopped and placed my forehead against the cool stone, begging my basilisk to go away. Kai caught up to me as I tried to control my breathing counting to ten over and over in my head. I could feel the scales pushing forward more as I began to smell Kai's scent.

My tongue flicked out and forked and I began to feel my scales pop out on my chest and back. Kai's heat touched my back softly and I screamed as my basilisk forced her way out. Kai's own hiss accompanied his forced shift as I slid towards the corner of the walls, forcing my basilisk in the opposite direction of the one

she wanted. Kai followed slowly, whispering for me to take steady breaths.

His larger body came into view and he froze; my basilisk preened as his eyes traveled from nose to tail. I felt my body rear up slightly before rolling onto my side showing my cloaca, of all things, and I could feel my embarrassment. "Sssstop, please," I begged myself, as I rolled more practically inviting Kai to fuck me here and now. Kai didn't come any closer, but his mouth opened like he could smell me.

I begged her to go away but she wouldn't budge. "Sssshe doessssn't want to lissssten," I cried out, as Kai moved closer to me slowly.

"Ssshe isss you," he said, as he curled around himself. I could see his hemipenes, signaling how aroused he was, but he ignored it and just waited.

My basilisk hissed her disappointment at him, for not taking advantage of her offer, and began to recede letting me take my human form once more. I was naked when I shifted back, and so was Kai, when he finally changed back as well. I couldn't help but stare at his cocks both of which were rock hard. Licking my lips, I looked up at the sky, as he laughed. "You might wanna look your fill now, since tonight we will all be naked."

"What? Why would we all be naked?" I asked horrified, looking back at Kai swiftly.

"Well sugar, you invited the Nymphs here, and custom dictates everyone who partakes in the meal must be naked." His explanation was offhanded, like it was no big deal to him. He walked closer and I pressed my back to the warm wall, until his warmer chest touched mine. I could feel both his cocks cradled against my stomach and I shivered slightly. He bent slightly and scooped me up under my knees before carrying me towards the bedroom. "None of us will touch you in either form without your consent," he whispered just before the doors opened, the guards averting their eye to give us privacy.

Once we made it to the bedroom, Kai slid me down his body and backed me towards the wall, between his door and Sic's. "Just because I won't fuck you without your permission doesn't mean I won't steal a kiss." He pressed his lips to mine, and I could feel every hard inch of his body pressed to my front. My body responded unbidden, and I opened my mouth when he slid his tongue along the seam in my lips.

Without warning, he picked me up and somehow my legs ended up wrapped around his waist as he carried me towards the bed. I could smell the desire he was giving off, and it was only increasing my own. I broke our kiss with a gasp, and he gently laid me in the bed, crawling up next to me. Instead of taking things further, he pulled the covers back and slid me in before covering me up. "We do need to talk about tonight, and you being naked is somewhat of a distraction," he whispered, as he slid next to me on top of the covers.

"Do we really have to be naked?" I asked, cringing at the thought.

"Unfortunately, yes, although you can wear a sheer dress and get away with it. Nymphs don't wear clothing, ever, so it would be an insult to go dressed in anything nontransparent. We

have had their King to functions in the past, however, he conformed to the customs dictated by the guest of honor. Since he is the guest of honor this time, it is only right that we bow to his customs," Kai trailed his finger along my collar bone, as he spoke. Something told me he was unaware of what he was doing.

I shifted slightly to face him, the cover slipping to expose my breasts. His gaze traveled down, and I could see how the sight affected him. Something inside me wanted to just reach out and touch him. "You can touch me," he whispered into my hair as he slid somewhat closer. His hand drew lazy circles along my shoulder, as he began kissing my forehead and face.

"I shouldn't. We need to discuss tonight more." I tried desperately to keep my hands to myself, but his chest was too close not to touch.

"There really isn't more to say, we all just have to deal with the repercussions of this dinner. Tonight is going to be interesting, and I suspect frustrating for all of us," his cryptic words brushed across my lips, as my hand settled on his chest. He slid my hand down his muscles, until it rested on his toned belly; leaving the rest for me to discover at my own pace. His mouth captured mine once more as his own hand slid towards my chest.

He avoided touching my aching peaks and slid his hand between my boobs before wrapping it around to my hip. He pulled back to look me in the eyes, "You know, there are other things we can do that don't require mating." Heat raced to my lower body at his suggestive words and I shivered in need.

Despite only knowing them for a short time, I couldn't deny the sexual tension I had been feeling, or the lust they all incited. I wanted to fuck them like no other, but the idea of it binding us together in wedded bliss scared the hell out of me. My hand slid an inch further down, until my wrist bumped into his

cocks. Holy shit, they were long, and they both had a fair amount of girth from what I had seen, I could only imagine what it would look like if he combined them.

"Do you want me to leave?" he asked, pulling away from my lips. His hand patiently waiting on my hip.

"No. I'm just not used to two cocks is all." I looked into his eyes for a second before blushing slightly and looking down. Big mistake since I looked right at where my hand was rested.

"Do you want me to make them one? Would that be easier for you?" He rolled slightly towards his back more, giving me a clear view of his body. My mouth watered at the sight, and I squeezed my thighs tight to alleviate the need some. I didn't know how to answer that, the idea of two cocks was a novel one, but I was somewhat curious about what they would look like once combined.

He seemed to understand my indecision and wrapped his hand around mine, sliding them both towards his crotch. My hand slid around the base of one as he grasped the other. Both were identical in every way and I could barely get my hand around his base. He kept still and quiet, letting me dictate what I did, and all I could think to do was slide my hand up.

His own hand mimicked my movement, and I could see him biting his lower lip, keeping himself in check. My hand slid back down and then his wrapped around mine again pulling my hand away. While I watched, he closed his eyes, and then both cocks began to knit together almost as if being sewn. My eyes bulged as his girth increased two-fold and he was even longer than before, damn near as long as my arm.

Once the two became one, he replaced my hand around his base, my fingers barely wrapping half. This monstrosity of a

cock scared the shit out of me, and yet, I was almost excited to see if it would even fit. Sliding my hand towards the head, it twitched in my grasp, and Kai let out a soft moan. "Sorry, one is twice as sensitive as two."

I marveled at how long he was, and his girth was almost frightening. Without warning he pulled my hand away, hissing as he reigned himself back in. "If you keep going, I'm gonna cum, and that isn't what I want right now."

"What do you want right now?" my voice sounded almost flirty as I asked, and he rolled back towards me. His eyes were filled with need and I began to ache deep in my core.

He rolled more so that I was on my back and he was cradled between my legs, the thin sheet the only thing keeping us apart. "What I really want is to make you cum, hear you scream in pleasure, but..." he trailed off, as I pressed my lips to his, arching so my nipples rubbed his chest.

When I pulled back his eyes were hooded and I could see a hint of fang, peaking trough his lips. "Do you want me to touch you?" his question was so soft, I barely heard it. Instead of answering with words, I pulled his hand up my side until his large palm cupped my breast.

I wasn't small in the bust department, but his strong hand could easily touch almost all of my tit. His thumb stroked my nipple and I groaned as it sent pleasure rippling down to my clit. "You have to answer my question, my Queen." I didn't want to speak, I only wanted to feel; let my mind go blank and forget the last few days, even if just for a moment.

"Please," I whispered, feeling my cheeks flush.

"Do you want me to make you cum?" This time his hiss was darker more commanding, and I could feel the wetness gathering between my legs.

I refused to answer as his thumb rubbed my nipple rhythmically, sending jolts of pleasure downwards. "You have to answer me, or I won't go any farther." His lips pressed to my neck and he kissed his way towards my lonely nipple. Blowing hot air across it before looking back up at me expectantly.

I closed my eyes as he toyed with my nipples. He suddenly pinched one between two fingers, firmly but not hard enough to hurt. My eyes flew open as I cried out, pleasure racing along my skin. "Yesss," I hissed, my basilisk drawing out the s sound.

Once the word crossed my lips, I felt his tongue swirl my other nipple and he massaged my other breast. I couldn't help but arch into his mouth more as his fangs grazed my areola. He rocked his hips once pressing through the sheets and groaned, the sound sending vibrations through my hardened bud. He released my nipple with a pop and looked up at me. "You're so wet, the sheet is soaked." I blushed in embarrassment as he lifted himself up and pulled the sheet away, devouring my body with his eyes.

His hand trailed down from my chest towards my pussy, and I arched as he neared. "Patience, sssugar," he said as my body begged for his touch. I watched as he recaptured my nipple and felt his forked tongue wrap around it. The sensation new and intense. While he distracted me with his tongue, I felt his hand slowly trail down my leg lifting it, so my foot was flat on the bed.

His hand slid back towards my core, and I cried out as he gently ran a finger along my slit. He circled my clit softly before breaking away from my nipple and kissing his way lower. Fingers continued to tease my pussy before he slowly slid one finger into me. I arched off the bed as he curled it and began to slowly thrust.

Hot air wafted over my clit just before he lowered his mouth to lick me.

I felt my body tighten as his tongue surrounded my clit and began to move, the fork helping him hit all the nerves. He worked a second finger alongside the first and then began to increase his speed. They stroked my g-spot rhythmically until I began to feel pressure that felt like I had to pee. "Kai, stop. I need to go pee." I didn't want to embarrass myself or disgust him, so I begged him to give me a moment.

He lifted his gaze and I marveled at the change in his eyes, but his smile was what captivated me. His tongue flicked out as he smiled and kept pumping a bit faster. "You don't have to pee, trust me. Just relax and let it come, besides, we're snakes and that is how we mark our territory and our mates." His head dipped back down like he didn't care and then moved his fingers faster.

He deliberately pressed upward into my g-spot and his hooked fingers stroked me. My body desperately wanted the release and I began to feel drops of moisture coating Kai's hand. "That'sss it, cum for me." he hissed against my clit, as he worked his hand even harder. His mouth locked back onto my pussy just as I exploded. I felt my body clamp on his fingers and then gushed wetness all over his hand and face.

He growled in pleasure against my clit before sliding his hand out from between my legs, licking both fingers before lifting his head. His eyes were all basilisk and I could see tiny white scales dotting his brow. Licking his lips, he slid his body up mine and I about begged for him just to keep going, but instead, he covered me back up slowly.

He wrapped me in his arms and my boneless body gladly let him. I could feel the hard ridge of his cock against my hip and I wiggled slightly. "Sssstop, ssssweet or I'll cum," he hissed in my

ear, but I also wanted to make him cum like he had made me cum. Placing my hand on his chest, I slid it down to grasp the base of his large cock.

Sitting up, I let the sheet fall around my waist, and added my second hand so I could encircle his entire girth. I rose them both making him try to grasp my wrist, but I didn't let that stop me. Shifting to my knees I bent forward and licked the precum off his head. Combined as they were, there was no way I could get more than his head into my mouth, my jaw just didn't unhinge in human form.

His hips bucked as my mouth encased his head. I stroked down again with my hands tasting more precum. The salty sweet taste made me crave more, and I swirled my tongue around his head. "Fuck, ssstop I'm about to cum." His hand tangled in my hair as he tried to pull me off gently, but I ignored it and sucked harder while moving my hands faster still. His body bowed, pushing more of his cock into my mouth just as the first shot of cum coated my tongue. "Yesssss, oh fuck yesssss."

I sucked him as far down as I could while he shot his load into my throat. He pulled out of my mouth swiftly as a second round of cum shot from his cock. I gaped as he coated his lower belly in his essence, and I had swallowed just as much. "Did you just have two orgasms?" I asked, as I laid back down, drawing small circles in the cum on his abs.

"In a manner of speaking, yes. Two cocks two orgasms. If they are separate, then they both happen at the same time. If they are together, it's one after the other. I didn't think you would want to swallow that much." He pulled me into his side, capturing the hand that was drawing in cum. I pulled the sheet higher for warmth and then began to doze off.

"Oh no, you don't. We still need to discuss tonight." I yawned as he tilted my head up and placed a kiss on my lips.

"What more is there to talk about? I get it, we have to be naked." Putting my head on his shoulder again, I closed my eyes.

"Well, for instance, the men have many wives. They have no filter where sex is concerned, and they will most likely have sex at the dinner table. Nymphs, specifically the women, are highly sexual beings and they feel no shame in riding whatever cock is available." He paused for a moment. "Nymph men live very long lives, as do the women, but the men are rare, maybe one to every two hundred women. The King became the King because he was able to produce several male children."

I was trying to wrap my head around the whole sex at the dinner table when something dawned on me. "Wait, you said whatever cock is available. Does that mean they could potentially want yours, Sic's, or Emot's?" Sitting up slightly, I looked him in the eyes. "Well, does it?"

"Yes, potentially. However, they are aware that you are the Queen, and we are your mates. Will that stop them outright? No, but they will be less likely to try to cross that line," he explained, and my basilisk hissed her displeasure even at the idea.

I realized then that my reaction was not normal. It shouldn't bother me who they slept with, since I wasn't even sure I wanted them myself, but for some reason my basilisk abhorred the idea. "Sorry, I shouldn't sound so possessive. You're not even mine," I said, wrapping my arms around my legs and placing my chin on my knees.

"Maisie, we are yours, whenever you want to make us so." His arms wrapped around me and I felt the cum on his chest stick to my back.

"Did you really just get cum on my back?" I asked, as he started to laugh.

"Better than in your hair." He laughed harder and I hid my snickering in my knees.

Kai was just about to pull me back down to cuddle more, when the door opened and Sic walked in. "We have a problem."

20

Emot

I stood beside Sic with my mouth gaping at the sight of Maisie and Kai in bed, her body flushed with color. Kai's chest was covered in cum and I was so damn curious as to how it got there. Sic's words brought me back to the present and out of my thoughts, "We have a problem." I looked at his face and realized he was clenching his jaw.

"What's the issue?" Kai asked, while sliding to the edge of the bed. I could see he had combined his dicks, and desperately wanted to ask if they had mated, but kept my mouth shut.

"Vago has returned, our spies reported a portal being opened in the Northern Kingdom. They said Vago and another person came through, and then it closed," Sic filled them both in, and Maisie jumped up quickly. Her naked body had me hard as stone in an instant.

"Was it my mother they saw? Is she alive?" she asked, while walking to the end of the bed and hopping off. She was standing in front of us, and I could smell Kai's scent as she spoke, answering at least one of my questions.

"They were too far away to tell who came through beside Vago, his basilisk is distinctive. They said the other person was in human form," Sic spoke, trying to not stare down at her body.

Kai walked over and whispered into her ear and her eyes got really big before she blushed. The rosy flush made her even more beautiful in my opinion. "Excuse me, will you, it seems I need a shower before the Nymphs arrive." She stepped back slightly before turning and practically running to the bathroom.

"Wasss that cum on her back?" I asked, as Sic death stared Kai.

"Seriously! Did you really mate with her right before her first major diplomatic event? You could have at least waited until tonight," Sic hissed in a deadly whisper, after the door to Maisie's bathroom closed.

Kai held up his hand in a placating manner, but he had a shit eating grin on his face. "We didn't mate. All I did was eat her pussy," he said, and I though Sic was about to fucking punch him.

Instead, he pointed at his stomach and dick. "Then why, the fuck, are you covered in cum?" Sic yelled.

"I wasn't about to make her swallow two whole fucking loads," as soon as the words left Kai's mouth, Sic snapped and punched him.

Kai hissed and instantly changed into his basilisk form, Sic followed suit, and then the real fight began. I backed towards Maisie's bathroom door to block her in case she chose that moment to emerge. Sic struck first and Kai coiled tight to avoid his teeth. "What the fuck issss your problem?" Kai yelled, as Sic tried to bite him again.

"Thisss isssn't the Kai ssshow, it issss ssssupposssssed to be all of usss," Sic's hiss was more pronounced, as his anger rose. A tiny breeze tickled my neck as the door swung open behind me. I turned to keep Maisie in the bathroom, but her naked body distracted me long enough for her to duck under my arm.

"What are you two doing?" She yelled, and both men froze, Sic's mouth inches from biting Kai again. Kai had blood dripping from several puncture wounds, but I knew they would heal in a few hours.

Kai shifted back, his cocks no longer one, as Sic backed away from Maisie. She glared at him and he shrunk back to human form, his head down turned, his body just as much on display as Kai's. "I asked a question," she said, looking between the two.

"Sssic got jealousss of Kai becausssse he thought you two had mated. Kai mentioned you only giving him a blow job and that set Sssic off," I filled in Maisie, as the other two stood looking at me with murderous eyes. "What, I'm gonna take her sssside every time," I added, as they glared.

"Suck up," Kai whispered, and I cocked my head sideways, towards Maisie.

Sic turned and walked into his room removing himself from the situation, and Maisie went to follow. Kai walked towards his own room and I stopped her with a hand on her arm. "Let me take care of Sssic, just make ssssure Kai is alright and nothing isss bleeding that won't heal before dinner." She looked at Sic's door and then nodded.

Before she entered Kai's room, she paused. "Does it really matter in which order I mate with you?" her voice was soft, and her eyes looked truly worried.

"No, it doesssn't. Sssic hasss alwayssss been the leader, he'sss the oldessst at twenty-nine, and seemsss to think he needs to be first at everything," I said, as I turned the handle on Sic's door. Maisie walked into Kai's room and I stepped into Sic's, the cool darkness highlighting his mood perfectly.

I shut Kai's door and saw him standing by a mirror looking over his shoulder at a nasty gash on his back. "Are you alright?" I asked, as I walked closer to inspect the damage.

"I'll be fine." He winced as I touched his side near a long gash, the skin already knitting itself back together.

"Do you need a healer to help speed it along?" he looked at me as I asked, before softly smiling at me.

"Truly, I'll be fine in a few hours. You should go finish getting ready." He shooed me to the door, then back out into my room. "Thank you, for checking on me," with that said, he closed the door and locked it.

Emot walked out of Sic's room with a grim look on his face. "Is he okay?" He just shrugged his shoulders at my question, and then walked towards his own room.

Pausing by his open door he looked back over at me. "He'sss jussst jealoussss, and he feelsss ssstupid for how he reacted," he closed the door softly after his words were said, leaving me alone in the room.

"What the fuck?" I called out to the empty room. Shivering in the cool air I decided to just get dressed for now, and if need be, strip later. A knock sounded on the door, softly intruding on my scattered thoughts. "Yes," I called out, only to see Sage's head peek around the door cautiously.

"His Highness, Prince Sicrin, asked me to come make you an outfit for tonight. He thought you might be more comfortable with something, even if it was sheer." She spoke calmly, and yet I could hear a touch of nervousness in her voice.

"Sure, come on in. We can go into the closet and away from the men." Rolling my eyes at the thought of the guys, I opened the doors, and she gasped.

"Oh, my. You have a very large selection already," she marveled, as she walked around the room slowly.

"It's a pity I didn't choose any of it," I remarked, as she circled the massive room.

"Oh, but some of these are breathtaking." The reverence in her voice as she stroked a piece of silk made me smile. "Anyway, let's get you a dress made up for tonight's dinner." She twisted her hands in an odd way and dozens of bolts of fabric appeared on the floor near the pedestal in the center of the room.

"How did you... Did you just..." words escaped me, as she smiled up at me as she picked up a bolt of mint green organza, that shimmered in the low light.

"I have magic just like everyone in the West Kingdom, although mine is limited to sewing and fabrics. I believe Prince Sicrin is much like his mother, with respect to the portals. I'm unsure of what else he might be able to do." She pulled a large amount of fabric off before making a cutting motion and slicing it off without scissors.

"That is amazing and really cool to watch," she laughed at my words, and then pulled me to stand on the pedestal.

"Now, what kind of dress would you like? We can do light and summery, with a shorter hemline. Although, that won't be the proper attire for a formal dinner, the fact that you have clothes on, at all, is going to be odd." She twisted the fabric around my naked body showing me what she meant.

"I really don't have a preference on the dress, but I would like someone to talk to. Can I ask you a question?" She looked up from where she was tucking more fabric around my waist and smiled.

"Sure, what do you want to know?" She turned her focus back to the dress as I tried to figure out how to phrase my words.

"How do you know when is the right time to mate with someone? How is it done, is it just sex or is there more? Does marriage mean mating? Will consummating the marriage mean mating?" I rattled the questions off, as my brain formed them. Without my mother here, there wasn't really anyone else I could ask.

Her quiet laughter preceded her standing to look me in the eye. "Well, for instance, when Thuzo and I began to date, our basilisks began to develop a bond, much like dating as well. We knew we wanted to marry and have children, so he asked me to marry him, but we still needed permission from the Kings and you, to actually mate. Not because it is required, but because he lives here, and I didn't." She paused for a moment and then sighed. "I'm not doing a very good job explaining, let me start over."

She knelt down on the floor, so I sat next to her halting the dress making altogether as we talked. "Let me start with the easy one. No, sex does not mean mating. Yes, that is how you mate, but it is more complicated than two humans having sex." She picked at a roll of super sheer pink silk as she talked. "Mating is sex but it's in both forms, it's a bonding between human and basilisk, both. For example, Thuzo and I have had sex in human form, but not basilisk form. He wanted to wait to mate on our wedding night."

"So, potentially, I could have sex with any of them, and it wouldn't be considered mating?" She nodded in response to my question.

"Yes, however, your case is a bit different. If you have sex with one of them, that marriage is binding. If my knowledge of the Treaty is correct, it says any sexual act solidifies your union with the man as the said act was performed." She gave me a sympathetic smile, as I mulled over her words.

"But sex just makes the marriage legal, it doesn't actually mate us, right?" I was trying to clarify for myself what was what. "How do you know about the Treaty?" I asked realizing she knew about the 'must have sex' clause.

"It is public record, for everyone, that way every citizen knows that peace will one day be achieved." My face must have said all she needed to know, because she continued. "So, the overall answer to all your questions revolves around sex. Yes, you can have sex without mating, marriage and mating are separate. However, for you, sex will bind you to them even without mating. As for your first question, you just know when the time is right, your basilisk will be more than vocal about it."

"Like showing its underbelly, and... cloaca?" I whispered the last word super softly.

"Yes, that can be a definitive indicator of your basilisk's willingness to mate, but that doesn't mean you can't choose. The difficult part of having a human sexual relationship without mating is that your basilisk might not be willing to wait. In which case you inevitably end up mating." She pulled the pink silk up and then rose. "Stand up, let's get this dress made."

She pulled the green organza off and tossed it aside, before wrapping the pink silk gracefully over my body. I watched in the mirror as it covered me, but still showed my skin underneath. "Is there a way to maybe leave a bit more off the top?"

"What do you mean? Like expose your upper half but not the lower?" She thought about it a moment, then began adjusting the fabric once more. When she was finished, I gaped at myself in the mirror. The dress wrapped my waist falling to just below my knees in front while draping to a short train at the back. My entire upper half was exposed in the front, but silk ran up my back in ribbons to create a collar around my neck. The effect was both stunning and erotic.

I could still see my lower body through the silk, but it was shadowed by the folds in the fabric giving more hints of nakedness, without being fully naked. "What do you think?" Sage asked as she cleaned the fabric up with a flick of her wrist.

"It's breathtaking. Will it be suitable for tonight's guests, I know Kai said they would all be naked?" My eyes kept being pulled towards my tits on display, suddenly feeling overcome with nerves.

"You look wonderful, and they should understand that you went as comfortable as possible. They do know that not every race is nude all the time, but Nymphs being Nymphs, they want instant access to everything," she laughed as she said this, and I couldn't help but chuckle.

"Thank you, Sage, for everything," I spoke, as she began walking towards the door.

"You're welcome, Your Majesty," she said, pulling the door open. "You have three very naked men, awaiting you, and I suspect the Nymphs will be arriving soon." She waved goodbye, as she closed the door behind her.

I stood looking at my reflection for a moment longer, and realized I needed to do something with my hair. Pulling the blond curls up, I pinned them in place with the bobby pins on the vanity, leaving a few stray curls to fall to my shoulders, but not all the way down my back. Once done, I stood up straight and walked barefoot to the door. Fuck shoes, if I had to be nearly naked, well then, barefoot was the way to go.

Opening the door, I walked out with my head held high, and Sic about fell over. Kai's mouth dropped open like he was trying to catch flies, and Emot ignored them both, while walking up to me. "You look ravissshing. Ssshall we?" Holding out his arm to escort me, I couldn't help but notice both his cocks were hard.

We led the way down the stairs just as the guards opened the castle's large doors. A very naked Nymph King, his son, and ten beautiful women walked in, full-sized. He smiled as we approached and bowed low once I reached his side. "Your Majesty, you look lovely. Might I escort you from here?" This last question was more to Emot than me.

Emot relinquished my hand and the Nymph King and I walked into the great hall. The room was beautifully laid out with white tablecloths and china plates. It felt like my mother's Christmas dinner, only with lots more people. There were people stationed around the room, and several women holding pitchers.

The Nymph King walked me towards the head of the table and pulled my chair out. "How is it that I can understand you without the crown?" I asked softly, as he pushed my seat in.

His hearty laugh accompanied his words, as the others began to take their places at the table, "When we are in full Nymph form, we can only speak with other races through the crown. When in humanish form, we can actually speak normally, we understand you just fine in Nymph form, however, we cannot respond in anything but Nymphish." He took his seat on the side of the table, sitting across from his son.

"What do I call you, Your Majesties?" I asked both of them, as the serving girls began filling glasses.

"Oh, my name is Nysali, but you can call me Ny. This is my eldest son, Hyllis." The pride in his voice was evident when he said eldest son, and I remembered that male Nymphs were rare.

"If you don't mind me asking, how many sons do you have?" He smiled as the servers began to bring out large platters of roasted veggies and raw fruits. One platter was covered in nothing but what looked like seaweed.

Once all the plates were deposited, Emot spoke up from his seat down the table. "We took the liberty to do this family-style so that you could all choose what you would like to eat. There will also be several delicate fish platters, if you so choose," Ny smiled as Emot spoke, and waved his hand for everyone to begin.

"At present, I have eleven sons, and seventy of my wives are currently in various stages of pregnancy. I have three thousand three hundred and eight nine daughters." I felt my eyebrows lift at hearing how many daughters he had. He laughed heartily as he noticed my face, placing some seaweed and roasted asparagus on

his plate. "Nymphs are a prolific lot, and when you have a thousand wives, well, many children are going to happen." He laughed once more and then offered me the seaweed. "It smells wonderful, as if it was prepared the way we do it."

"Emot prepared the meal, Your Majesty," I spoke, as I took a small bite, I had never eaten seaweed but didn't want to offend our guests, so I would try some.

"Oh Tsk. It's Ny, since this is to be a family style dinner let us not stand on formality Margaret," he spoke happily, as he took small bites of food. "I do hope your Emot has planned octopus, it has been many years since I have had it prepared the basilisk way, and it is by far my favorite."

"Please call me Maisie," I spoke, while looking to Emot. His slight nod had me turning back to the King with a smile. "I do believe it was prepared, and if you would like, we can have it brought out." I took a sip of my drink and strange bubbles shot up my nose making me sneeze. "Pardon me."

"No need, the fizzy Sprite makes me sneeze too sometimes." He took his own sip before continuing to enjoy his food. I picked up my fork and stabbed a small piece of seaweed and placed it in my mouth. The texture was odd but not unpleasant, and the flavor was out of this world. It had a distinctly Asian flavor with a mellow sweetness that was a perfect foil for the vinegary taste. The rest of the table talked as we ate with conversations about everything from mating rituals to human movies.

I drank two more glasses of the Sprite, before realizing I was feeling somewhat odd. My tongue felt thicker, and the room was tilted ever so slightly. I watched one of the Nymph women duck down under the table for a moment, and then heard a bang on the underside. I couldn't help but duck down, only to see her

bobbing her head up and down the Prince's cock. Blushing, I sat back up and downed my third glass of Sprite. "I thought this was a soda, why do I feel funny?"

Sic laughed at my question, as two men brought out a mass platter of octopus and placed it in the center of the table. "Sprite isn't a soda, it is called that because it is a fizzy wine brewed by the Sprites. Did you know Sprite means spirit, and Sprites brew spirits?" He laughed at his bad joke causing me to realize I wasn't the only one who probably had more than enough.

Ny gleefully rubbed his hands together as the server carved a large portion of octopus off for him. Placing it before him, and a second plate in front of me, he smiled and yelled, "Dig in!" I cut a small bite of the tentacle off and popped it into my mouth. I had tried more new foods tonight than in all my life, and even this was amazing.

I watched the others devour their portions as the King asked for seconds. "Did you know the combination of seaweed and octopus is an amazingly wonderful aphrodisiac?" My fork clattered to my plate as one of his wives rose and walked towards the end of the table only to sit in his lap. I think my eyes bugged out when she began to rise and fall while he continued to eat bites.

Another woman crawled under the table and Emot jumped up swiftly as a hand tried to follow. "Your Majesty, I am aware that it is custom, but I would prefer to refrain, if only out of difference to my Queen." The others repeated the sentiment, just as the woman bouncing on the king's lap moaned. I could feel the blush on my face as I tried to ignore what was going on next to me.

He pushed her off his lap as he went for thirds on the octopus. "No offense taken." He said something I couldn't

understand and the woman who had been on the floor rose and took the now-vacated lap of the king. By the time dinner was over all five of his women had ridden the King and the same with his son. My blush was so intense even my breasts were red, and the room was almost spinning from the drinks I had consumed.

It was late into the night before the King and his family left, but they seemed in very good spirits. Kai had to help me stand as the alcohol went to my head. Once they were gone, Emot and Sic disappeared upstairs singing oldies from Earth, and leaning heavily on one another.

I swayed a bit until Kai scooped me up and began to head towards the stairs. "Wait. I would like some fresh air," I slurred, causing him to change his direction towards the courtyard.

"Are you alright?" he asked, as he sat down on the same stone bench we had been on this afternoon.

"I think so, just a bit tipsy," I said, while looking into his blue blue eyes.

"Thankfully, the Sprite doesn't last long, now the giants brew is an ale that will have you drunk for a week, if you drink too much." He tucked me close to his chest, keeping me warm. His naked skin tantalizingly close.

I traced my hand along the chiseled plane of his chest, until his hand captured mine. "Please don't, because I know that we have both had too much to drink."

I sighed in disappointment. "But what if it's what I want. Not the whole mating thing, but just normal human sex."

"For one, I can't guarantee that a mating won't take place, not in my current state. For two, I won't take advantage of you

like that. For three, I think the only reason you want anything sexual is because you just spent an entire dinner watching Nymphs have sex. They don't call it nymphomania for nothing," Kai's words burst my bubble faster than a pin pops a balloon.

Pushing out of his lap, I stood, finally steady on my feet once more. "Why is it so wrong to want sex? Also, why is nymphomania such a bad thing, men aren't chastised for their sexual urges, or for being satyriasis?" I paced along the path not paying attention to where I was walking, fully expecting Kai to respond to my comment. Turning a corner, I heard my basilisk hiss, and then an arrow whizzed by my face. If she hadn't stopped me, it would have hit me right in the temple. "KAI!" yelling, I turned and ran back towards the main doors and where I had last seen him. He scooped me up, swiftly running inside. It wasn't until we were safely inside that I saw an arrow sticking out of his shoulder.

The guards swarmed around us, before pulling me away from Kai. They rushed me up the stairs to my room and formed a wall across my door after pushing me inside. Kai was still downstairs, with an arrow sticking out of him. "Sic, Emot," I called out, as I opened the bedroom door. Kai and Emot's doors were open but Sic's was closed. Rushing over I opened it without knocking and got an eye full.

Sic was holding on to Emot's throat as he pounded into him from behind, Emot moaning as he worked his own cocks. "Excuse me," I said, and began to close the door once more when Emot's loud hiss had me turning back. My basilisk basking in the pleasure she could see on their faces distracted her from the emergency at hand. Emot locked eyes with me and groaned as both cocks shot cum across the covers of Sic's bed.

He slumped forward onto his hand and that's when Sic noticed me standing there. It was too late to beat a hasty retreat, so I turned around, giving them privacy, even if only a little. My basilisk hissed at me menacingly for not watching more, and I reminded her about Kai. "What do you want?" Sic's voice was rough but not unkind.

"Kai was shot with an arrow." Glancing back over my shoulder, I noticed Sic pause. Emot cursed and then I could hear feet hitting the floor. I jumped out of the way as Sic's naked body raced by me, only to hit Emot square in the chest.

His arms wrapped around me from behind and then he closed the door. "Stay here. Our rooms have no windows, there is also a hidden passage under Sic's bed in case you need to flee. Lock the door until you hear one of us." He pointed me towards the floor under the bed, before racing off after Sic. Locking the door, I grabbed Sic's robe to cover my exposed breasts, then huddled in a chair beside the bed.

I must have dozed off because a knock on the door startled me to the point that I fell out of the chair and hit the floor hard. I brushed myself off as I walked to the door. "Yes?" I asked, but no reply came from the other side. A second knock sounded and again I asked, "Yes?" Someone tried the doorknob, before swiftly kicking the door. The wood held firm as I rushed to the bed and crawled under it. Feeling around for the door Emot had spoken of I flinched as the door was kicked again.

My basilisk hissed as my finger brushed a crack in the floor and I wedged my finger into it. Pulling up the small trap door, it moved silently on well-oiled hinges. I shimmied myself over the opening and realized the only way I would survive a fall that far was to shift. I let my basilisk take over and shifted, uncomfortably filling the space beneath the bed. The sound of splintering wood had me moving faster than anything else and I slithered down the hole, hearing the room door slam against the far wall as the trap door fell silently closed.

Coiling my body tight, I hit the ground and hissed in slight pain. Flicking my tongue out I could smell fresh air off to my left and twisted to face the path. The darkness was all-encompassing, as I moved down the path. My mind trying to ignore the

possibilities of real snakes and spiders. Slithering faster to get away from this dark hole, I began to hear running water.

The last hundred feet of the tunnel were somewhat slimy, and light began to permeate the darkness. I tried to ignore the feel of nastiness on my belly as I continued to make my way toward the exit. Rounding the last bend in the pipe, I broke free into the fresh air, only to realize I had no idea where I was. There was a small gold lake with a high waterfall off to my left, so I slithered into the pool to rinse off before shifting back into human form. Once clean and walking again, I worked myself up to a higher position so I could get a better view of my location.

High above me on the top of the cliff was the castle. I could barely make out the guards rushing around the outer walls. I almost fell when I heard a soft feminine voice speak. "Why are you hiding, basilisk?" There were two glowing green eyes staring at me from the golden pool of water.

"Who are you? How did you get here?" I asked, while looking for other people.

"My name is Indra; I am the liaison of the Merqueen's." She slid out of the water and I noticed her shimmering teal tail. "As for how I got here, I live here in the pool, as an attaché to the basilisk Princes, to foster good relations between our kind and yours. Who are you?"

"My name is Margaret or Maisie," I had barely gotten the words out, when she gasped and bowed low.

"I am so sorry Your Majesty, I did not realize. Please forgive me," she remained bowed low as she spoke.

"Please don't, Indra. You don't need to bow to me," reassuring her, as I slowly climbed back down towards the water.

"Why are you so far from the castle? The only ones who come to speak with me normally are one of the Princes," she asked, as I sat next to her on the large rock she had surfaced on.

"Well, to be honest, someone broke into the castle and shot Kai with an arrow, Emot told me to hide in Sic's room, and that there was an escape route. I heard someone kicking at the door, so I ran and ended up here." I shivered in the cool air as a breeze blew across my naked skin.

"Oh dear, you must be chilled, come follow me." She pulled me back towards the water and dove in pulling me with her. Her lips pressed to mine and I realized she was blowing air into my lungs. She swam off towards the bottom of the pool and through a small opening, pausing once to give me air once more.

We resurfaced in a small cave that was dimly lit with a fire, and a man sat rocking a small bundle. Indra surfaced next to me and climbed out of the water, as I noticed her tail had split into two legs, covered in scales. "Come, warm yourself. This is my mate Wade and our son Trent. We won't tell anyone you are here, and we will know as soon as someone else touches the pool."

Accepting her offer, I climbed out of the water and sat next to the fire, Wade was rocking the small child as Indra grabbed me something warm to wrap around myself. "Would you like some tea? We have Kelp, Posidonia, and Seaweed."

"Umm... I guess whichever is sweetest." The oddity of the types she offered threw me for a loop, but I didn't want to offend. "May I ask why you two live here? I know you said you were an ambassador of sorts, but why not still live in the mermaid city, or whatever you have?"

Wades' soft chuckle brought my attention to his kind face. "Atlantis has been somewhat tumultuous of late. The Queen has been gone for almost thirty years and the regent who is currently in charge has seen fit to crown himself the new king, in her absence. He is nothing more than a tyrant, so when Indra was offered this position four years ago, we took it. It has given us a safe place to grow our family. We also have a three-year-old daughter, Maryn. Besides, it is a two days swim to or from, so we couldn't live there and still do this job," his voice was soft, as if he was trying not to wake the baby in his arms.

Indra walked over and handed me a shell cup filled with a greenish liquid. "This is Posidonia tea, it is a wonderful antioxidant and the flavor is by far the sweetest." I tentatively took a sip and tried not to gag as warm briny water slid down my throat.

"Thank you," my words brought a smile to her face, as she took the bundle from Wade and carefully placed it into a beautiful shell basinet. The natural curve hugged the baby as he slept.

"You don't have to drink it. We won't be offended in the slightest, Indra tends to put too much salt in hers, I prefer mine without salt," Wade spoke, allowing me to place the cup on the ground.

"Oh, I completely forgot Wade, this is Her Majesty, Margaret." His eyes bugged wide at Indra's words and I could tell he was about to bow when I stopped him.

"Please don't, Maisie is fine, and there is no need to bow. Thank you both for allowing me to stay here for a bit." I tried to hide a yawn behind my hand after I spoke but failed.

"Would you please take our bed? It is cozy and warm, and we will keep watch for anything suspicious while you get some rest," Indra spoke while helping me stand.

I wasn't given much choice as she tucked me in between warm covers. "Thank you," I whispered, as my eyes slowly slid closed.

23

Maisie

A shaking sensation woke me out of a deep sleep, but the darkness in the room didn't allow me to see what was going on. "Your Majesty." The memories from the night before flooded my brain and I sat up with a start. A gentle hand pressed to my shoulder, making me look up into Indra's glowing eyes. "Your Majesty. Prince Sicrin is at the edge of the pool. Should I send him away or not?"

I knuckled the sleep from my eyes and began to rise. "No, I should go back. I don't want to put you and your family at risk. Thank you for being so kind to me, and if you ever need anything, please let us know." We walked to the edge of the pool and Indra jumped in first. I dropped the blanket, waved goodbye to Wade, took a deep breath and followed her into the water.

Indra gave me a breath about halfway in, and then pulled us up behind the waterfall. She left me for a moment to speak to Sic. I couldn't make out his words with the rushing water. I realized she was making sure it was really Sic before handing me back over, still protecting me if she could. She popped back up next to me a moment later. "It is Prince Sicrin, if you want to go back..." she trailed off, as I hugged her.

"Thank you for helping me, and I hope one day I will be able to come back and visit." I pulled out of her arms and she nodded.

"You will always be welcome, and during the day the kids play in the pools, so you are welcome to come back and visit anytime." She pulled me under the water and then we popped back up in the pool, the sunlight just beginning to lighten the sky. Sic's eyes were filled with relief as I surfaced, and then he was pulling me into his arms as soon as I was back on solid ground.

Indra ducked back under the water and disappeared, about the time Sic loosened his grip ever so slightly. Before I could protest, he scooped me up and began walking back towards the gap in the cliffs I had slid through, only hours before. He didn't set me down until we reached a small path that led towards an open field. Backing me up until I was under an overhanging rock, he pressed his naked body along mine. Sparks lit my nerves as his large body shielded mine from the chilly morning air.

"I know I'm not Kai, but... fuck..." he broke off his words, as he smashed his mouth to mine. My basilisk purred her approval as his tongue slid along the crease between my lips. Tentatively opening for him, he slowed the intensity of our kiss, making love to my mouth with his. I could feel his cocks pressed against my stomach, and it took everything I had not to climb him like a tree.

I pulled back first, gasping for breath as his lips traveled down my chin to my neck. "Sic... I don't wanna mate." He paused for a moment and then continued kissing my shoulder.

"Who said anything about mating?" He lowered to his knees slowly kissing down between my breasts. Flicking his tongue along my tightened buds as he went. My head fell back against the rough stone as he trailed kisses down my stomach

stopping just before the v of my thighs. His breath was warm, contrasting with the cool air on the rest of my body.

My moan echoed around us as he finally laved my clit with his tongue. He picked up my leg and draped it over his shoulder in an attempt to get to all of me. I threaded my fingers into Sic's hair as he began to flick and suck, alternating between hard and soft motions. My pussy ached to be filled, the need pushing all rational thought and care from my mind. "Sic, please. I need more," I begged, as he worked me closer to that sweet release.

His fingers slowly circled my entrance as he pulled his face away. "What do you want, tell me, and I'll give you anything." I know what he was asking, but I couldn't bring myself to say it. He slid a finger deep and my body clenched around it, greedily begging for more. Lifting my head, I looked down my body only to realize he was staring up at me. There was something in his eyes that told me he wanted more as well but was holding himself in check.

My mind went over all the consequences and decided to say fuck it. I pulled my leg off his shoulder, lowering myself to his lap. His finger continued to work me as I captured his mouth once more. I could feel both his cocks and honestly wondered how that would work in human form. Gasping, he pulled back. "You have to tell me what you want."

I shook my head no, not wanting to say the words out loud. His hand stilled leaving me so close to that sweet release I craved. I whispered words from my lips, as I squeezed my eyes closed, "I can't." What, I didn't even know at this point, I couldn't say the words or couldn't sleep with him, my brain wouldn't focus.

"I think we should go back before we do something stupid," he spoke, as he flicked his thumb over my clit one final time, sending me spiraling. His chuckle mixed with my cries, as he

slid his hand free, standing back up without setting me down, my legs wrapped around his waist, my head buried in his shoulder. The sun was rising higher as he began walking towards the open field below.

When we made our way off the rocky path, I felt a soft blanket draped over my back and raised my eyes to Emot's soft smile. A carriage waited just to one side of the path, and Sic strode straight for it. The door opened as we neared, and he stepped inside followed by Emot. The darkness inside was soothing, and I heard Emot whispering to someone, but couldn't hear the words.

Turning my head, I peeked out and saw Kai sitting on the far side of the carriage next to Emot. His shoulder had a bandage covering the place the arrow had been, but he looked fine. He smiled softly as the carriage clattered through the castle gates. Once we rolled to a stop, the door opened, allowing Emot and Kai out. Sic rose slowly, working his way out of the carriage without jostling me too much. The second we were out of the carriage he was striding into the castle and up the stairs.

Emot sat with me next to the fire as Sic disappeared into the bedroom area. A worker was removing wooden door pieces from the bedroom area, ignoring Emot and Me sitting by the fire. Emot pulled me close and kissed my head, making sure I was wrapped up nice and warm. "I'm glad you're sssafe. When we came back into the room and our doorsss were busssted in, we knew sssomething had happened. Whoever it was essscaped off the balcony in here," I curled closer to his warmth, as he spoke.

"I used the escape tunnel you told me about. Then I met Indra and she let me stay with her for the night," I spoke softly,

142

not wanting to disturb the peaceful air in the room. "Was it the same person who shot Kai?"

He wrapped an arm around me, pulling me closer still. "No, we caught the man who ssshot at both of you. He wasss jussst hired for the Nymph dinner asss extra protection and admitted that he wasss only supposssed to ssscare you. He issss being held in the dungeonsss at the moment, for more quessstioning."

"What about the man who kicked the door down?" I asked, shivering slightly as I remembered.

"We don't know who the other one wassss, and after he found the roomsss empty, he fled," Emot spoke softly, but there was something he wasn't saying.

"Tell me." I sat up and looked him directly in the eyes.

"The sssecond man wasssn't a basssilisk sssshifter. He sssmelled of an avian variety ssshifter, Vulture to be ssspecific. They live acrossss the Calsssend Sssea on Dupradale, we don't typically sssee their kind here," he explained, while pulling the blanket higher around my shoulders. "It sssssuggests that he wasss hired to take you. Thuzo issss currently going through all the guard'sss recordsss, checking to verify their connectionsss." He pulled me back into his embrace and I snuggled into his warmth.

The cozy fire coupled with Emot's heat made me yawn, but I needed to stay awake, there was no telling what might happen next. Emot pulled me further into his lap making sure I was directly in front of the flames. "You need sssleep, yesssterday wasss long and I doubt you got much in Indra'sss place. Do you want me to tuck you in?" I yawned again as he asked, prompting him to cradle me as he stood.

Emot rushed the workers away as he carried me to the large bed. He knelt so he could place me in the middle and then pulled the covers up over my body. Just as he began to slide back, I reached out and grabbed his hand. "Please stay. I don't want to be alone." He smiled softly, before laying down next to me. His warmth, aided by the comfort of the soft mattress, had me drifting back off to sleep within minutes.

Hissing woke me up as Emot's body tightened around mine, not hard enough to suffocate me, but I was definitely under a very large basilisk body. I pushed Emot's scales trying to get out from under him, but he wouldn't loosen his grip. My basilisk hissed causing him to look down at me, and then shift enough to let me get free. "What the hell Emot?" I asked, and then saw Viper standing in the doorway.

"He seems to think I mean to harm you. I have news. So, if you would be so kind as to call off your guard snake," her sarcastic words had me chuckling.

"Emot, she isn't going to hurt me, and I doubt she knows what happened here. If she does, she might have useful information. Where are Sic and Kai?" I asked, as he slowly uncoiled his protective death grip.

"They are ssstill interviewing the prisssoner," Emot hissed, while shifting back into human form.

"Viper, could you give us a moment? To dress and get the others up here, unless what you need to say is pressing." She smiled, bowed, and closed the doors behind her as she left.

Emot turned to face me, his eyes dropping to my chest. "I'll go let the othersss know, while you get dressssed." As he rose,

I noticed both his cocks were hard and I couldn't help but smile a touch. I hadn't even kissed the man, and yet, this desire for all of them was becoming more of an issue as the days passed. When I first arrived, all I had wanted was to get home. Now, I wasn't quite sure what I wanted.

I watched Emot leave the room and slid from the bed. Walking to the bathroom, I pulled the robe of the hook. Pulling it on, I opened the double doors and saw Viper's disappointed face. "Awe, I was hoping to see you naked again." I smiled as I sat on the couch and she slid next to me. "You smell like desire. I wonder who has caused that, Emot, Kai, Sic? Maybe all three."

My blush made her laugh harder, but not unkindly. "I don't know what to do. I feel this connection to each of them, but I don't want to mate," I said, as she smirked.

"Then don't mate. You're the Fucking Queen of Lasina. Tell them what you want and how you want it. Start acting like a Queen," her voice was strong, as if she were trying to empower me, to fire me up, and it was working.

The door swung open as she leaned closer. "Wanna see what a worked up male basilisk will do? Maybe after I tell you the news, I'll help you." She turned towards the guys as they all walked closer. "Nice of you to join us."

"You said you had news?" Sic asked, as he eyed Viper warily.

Viper turned and looked at the guys for a moment; Emot's eyes flashed to mine as his mouth dropped open. She smiled as she looked back at me and winked before speaking. "Zugo is strong enough to make it to the Northern Coast, so you need to make an extraction plan. You will have two days more to figure it out and then we will need to move." She paused to look at the

guys Emot's mouth still hanging open. "I also know who hired the distraction, and the thief."

"Vago hired the man to shoot at Maisie, that much I know.," Sic said, crossing his arms over his chest.

"Yes, but he also hired the thief to look for something, and if possible, bring Her Majesty back to him. His name is Vathis, he's a vulture shifter. From what information I could gather, he was exiled for killing his entire nest. Let's just say the rest of his deeds shouldn't be repeated in front of Her Majesty but he is a vulture." Viper rose from the couch before turning back to me. She bent forward and pressed a chaste kiss to my lips before pulling back. "Enjoy your evening," her whisper was barely audible, as she shifted into her snake form and slithered out.

Sicrin

I turned as Viper slithered out the doorway and disappeared as if invisible, wondering if she really was half human. Something just didn't sit right with me, and yet, I couldn't put my finger on it. Her ability to materialize and disappear was too good to be just snake instincts, but then again, basilisks were large creatures and while they shared traits, they weren't snakes. "Kai, let's go, we need to see what else we can get out of that guard. We also need to make sure none of the other guards are being bribed. Emot. Emot. Emot." I snapped my fingers in front of his face, but he just stood gaping at Maisie.

Pulling his face towards mine, he snapped his mouth shut. "What?"

"You need to keep Maisie safe. Don't leave her side, even for a second," I spoke, and he just gulped and nodded. "Let's get this over with so we can plan on how to get Zugo back." Kai and I walked out the door, closing it behind us.

"What was his issue?" Kai asked, and I shrugged.

"I have no clue. Maybe he doesn't like Viper, maybe he was daydreaming about Maisie, who knows?" We walked down the stairs and headed towards the 'dungeon', and that is putting it

vaguely. The jail cells were outside of the castle, well away from our Queen, just in case a prisoner escaped.

We walked down the rocky path to the lower barracks, and then down into the block of cells. The cell where our prisoner was being held was only two down, but I could already smell the blood. I looked between the bars and saw our captive, slumped over with an arrow through his chest. "FUCK!" Kai yelled, as he saw the mess.

"There is someone else here working for Vago," whispering, just in case someone was listening. "We need to find them. Thuzo should be able to help us sniff out the traitor."

"Let's go see what he knows, also a trip to see Ahxezo and Yaga might help us in our search. They seem to know more than they let on," Kai's words made sense, those two old coots had eyes everywhere, and I was fairly sure Ahxezo used to be a spy for Kai's dad. We walked back out of the barracks and walked towards Thuzo's office.

The door closed on Sic and Kai, as Emot's gaze swung my way once more, the heat in his gaze scorching. "Did you really have sssex with Viper?" his words were hushed, as he prowled closer.

Rising, I backed towards the bedroom, as he continued to stalk my steps. "We might have, why do you ask?" I tried to play it off, but if he was asking then she must have given him his memories back.

I felt the back of my legs touch the bed as Emot closed the bedroom door. "Becaussse, I have the memory of her tail making you cum." My body clenched at nothing as he worked his way closer, the danger his body was conveying both nonthreatening and erotic. He stopped just shy of pressing his chest to mine and bent his head towards my neck.

Flicking his tongue out he trailed it up to my ear, nipping my lobe before whispering, "I can ssssmell your dessssire, and it'sss driving me mad." He lifted his head and was just about to step back, when I pulled his lips to mine.

The thin thread holding us back snapped and he lifted me by the waist. Breaking our kiss, he asked in a rough voice, "You

know what this meansss. We can ssstill ssstop." In answer, I pulled the tie off the robe and let it fall open slightly.

I screamed as he tossed me backwards onto the bed, only to have it turn into a moan as he trailed kisses up my ankle and calf. He stripped his own robe off as he slithered up my body exciting me more with each caress. I realized how desperately I needed this, when he pulled my robe aside further and then slipped a finger along my slit. Arching as his finger teased me, he worked two in and curled them to hit my g-spot.

"If you don't want thisss you need to ssstop me now, because, Godsss, I want you. I have been sssmelling you for days," he growled, just before his tongue slid up my clit, circling twice before pulling back. The look of ecstasy on his face had me trying to pull him up my body. "Oh no Princesss, you need to be ready if you're going to take all of me. Besssidesss, you need to tell me what you want, one or two, because it will make a difference."

I shook my head as he continued to work his fingers, not wanting to answer his question. He knelt up so I could see his full body including both cocks, proudly standing at attention. The beauty of snakes, no hair, not anywhere except head and face, and it made both his cocks look that much bigger. He pulled my hand to his cocks and asked once more. "Two?" My hand wrapped around both as he paused, "Or One?" I felt his cocks begin to shift and I realized he was just as big as Kai had been.

My mind blanked as he slid a third finger into my pussy and began to move just a bit faster. "I think we sssshould do one this first time." He bent forward and pressed his lips to mine and I felt a fourth finger slip in. His tongue mimicked his fingers, as my body greedily accepted everything he gave me. His thumb pressed my clit as he worked more of his hand in. "The beauty of a basssssilisk woman, sssshe can take anything her mate could give her. You could probably take four cocksss at once if you wanted,

and that issss fucking sssexy," his words sent a shiver up my spine, as I felt him working his thumb in alongside his other fingers.

He curled his fingers rhythmically, rubbing all sorts of nerves I never even knew existed, then he began to rotate his wrist and I cried out in pleasure. My body drew tight as he worked me, and the room began to spin as stars appeared behind my eyelids. When my eyes had fallen closed, I didn't know, but the pleasure was so intense, all I could do was let him pleasure me. He twisted his hand swiftly, and the stars exploded, flinging me into rapture.

I felt him hiss as he licked around his hand, knowing that I had probably made quite a mess, but not caring in the slightest. I needed more and my basilisk hissed her own pleasure at the idea. "Emot... I need... more," I tried to speak through my panting breath, but it still came out hushed.

He slowly pulled his hand from me, and rubbed his cock with my wetness, before positioning the massive head of his cock at my entrance. "We can sssstill ssstop," he spoke, as he held himself in check, waiting for me to make my choice.

I wrapped my legs around his hips trying to get him in me faster, but he didn't budge. "You have to sssay it Maissssie, it hasss to be your choice, becaussse once we do this, there isss no going back," Emot's words cooled some of my need. Was this really binding, here yes, but if I chose to go back to Earth would it still be? I realized I didn't care, I needed something, anything.

"Please Emot, just human form for now, I'm not ready for the rest," I said, and he bent to kiss me.

"That I can do." His words were punctuated with him sliding in, my body stretching to take every bit of his massive cock. Once he was fully seated, he lowered himself onto my chest

and then rolled us twisting my legs, so they didn't end up trapped beneath him. He lifted me up to my knees and the thrust up into me, his cock never leaving my body.

"Oh fuck," I cried out, as I sat up looking down at his body. The pleasure was beyond anything I had ever felt, even a vibrator failed to compare. I began to meet his thrusts with my own downward motions, and we were both groaning. Our pace picked up, until he sat up and I felt a forked tongue flick my nipple.

The rapid change in angle sent me over the edge again, and I screamed out as my body clamped around his. His own grunt was punctuated by the hot feeling of cum filling my pussy. He didn't stop though, and he wrapped his arms around me once more and flipped us back over. My legs were trapped between our chests, curled tight and he began to pound harder.

The spasms of my orgasm never stopped as he slammed into me rapidly, rolling his hips to hit both my g-spot and my clit. My body began to climb a second peak I didn't even know existed and then clamped tight on his cock, he couldn't move as my body held him deep and pulsed around the top of his cock. He swore as his cock once again filled me with cum and then we both collapsed. My legs wrapped around his hips as he tried to keep his weight off me, with his elbows.

"I'm going to roll usss until you relax, and I can ssslip out." He said, as he slowly rolled us so I was laying on his chest, my body sending more pleasurable spasms up my spine.

"Why can't you pull out?" I asked somewhat ignorantly, since this was the first time I had actually slept with another basilisk, and Sam had never had issues pulling out.

"Well, your body hasss clamped onto mine, it isss moving my cum most likely to the optimal place to ssstore it until you are ready to breed." He smiled as I placed my chin on his chest.

"Wait, are you saying that my body is basically storing baby gravy for later use? How is that even possible?" I felt my body tighten for a moment and then relax a bit more allowing his cock to finally slip free. I was fully expecting the weird feeling of cum along with it, but nothing else came out.

"Male basssilisssk sssperm can live for up to five yearsss, as long as it is kept in a female. The female can then choossse the right time to give birth, let'sss just sssay it isss an evolutionary remnant of being the product of a Norssse monsssster." He kissed my head before pulling the covers up our bodies, shielding me from the chilled room. "Like I sssaid the decisssionsss are all yoursss." He kissed my eyelids closed as he adjusted me, so I was more comfortable. "Now get sssome sssleep."

I couldn't seem to sleep even though I was fully relaxed after the amazing orgasms. My body craved more of him, but also, I had a strange desire to get to know the man I had just slept with. "Emot," I whispered.

"Hmmm?" I could hear the smile in his voice but didn't open my eyes to check.

"I realized I know very little about you. How old were you when you signed the Treaty?" I was curious, because if I remembered correctly, he had still been young.

"Sssic wasss nineteen, Kai wasss ssseventeen, and I wasss fifteen. Why?" he pulled me tighter into his side, as he spoke. "I don't regret it, you know. I would do it all over again." I peeked

up at him through slitted eyes at his words. He was staring up at the ceiling, caught in a memory.

I tilted my head up more so I could see all of his face, his stubble tempting me to run my hand along it. "Why did you sign it?" I asked, and he looked down at me and smiled.

"I'm the oldessst of four boysss. My mother hasss alwaysss dreamed of a country united. My father asss well, he took her dream asss his own when they mated. My parentsss' marriage was arranged when they were very young, but I think it wasss ssstill love at firssst sssight." He placed a hand under his head and looked at me. "I guesssss having them asss an example made me hopeful that my own marriage, even if arranged, could be the sssame."

I rolled more so I was laying on his chest fully once more. "Has this 'marriage' met your expectations?" I air quoted the word marriage as I sat up fully, feeling his cock stir again beneath me.

He swiftly flipped me over making me giggle. "I'd sssay I'm enjoying the perksss now, but waiting wasss hell." His lips pressed to mine as he rolled his hips. "Sssince you aren't asssleep, and I didn't wear you out... wanna go again?"

I wrapped my legs around his hips and pulled his lips back to mine. "What does two cocks feel like, I wonder?" I whispered against his lips, and he reached between us to line himself back up. He slowly slid back in and I moaned as his tongue mimicked his hips, slowly exploring my mouth.

Breaking our kiss, he lifted up onto his hand and rolled his hips. "Are you sssure you wanna have two?"

"Gods, yes," I moaned, as he began moving in a slow steady rhythm.

I slowly began to feel a stretching sensation as he let his cock split back into two. He kept his movements slow, but the fullness felt amazing as he drew back out. I moaned as he began to thrust faster, rocking against my clit as he pressed back in.

"What do you think of two? Do you want me to go back to one?" The insecurity in his words was sweet, but unnecessary.

"It feels... Oh God... amazing," I tried to speak, but the sensation was overwhelming my brain.

"Wanna feel sssomething really cool?" he asked as he pressed fully in, and then paused.

"What could feel better than this?" I asked breathlessly.

"Thisss." I felt his cocks shift back together and the split again. It felt like a swirling sensation but not, and it was beyond pleasurable.

He began to thrust again while repeatedly switching between two cocks and one. The adorable look of concentration on his face made me smile, as I pulled his head back down to mine. "Just fuck me please, however you want." I kissed him as he began to thrust harder, his cocks remaining separated.

He lifted my leg over the crook of his elbow, and I cried out as the angle pressed my g-spot more. "I wanna feel you cum on my cocksss," his naughty words sent tingles up my spine, and my body tightened around him. He picked my other leg up, so it rested on his arm as well, and I felt my body grow wetter.

"That's it love, cum all over my cocks." My body drew tight as he slammed into me. Without warning, I felt my body flood around his, then my pussy began spasming rapidly around

him. I screamed out my pleasure as he slammed one final time and grunted as he followed me over the edge.

Emot lowered my legs back down and pressed his forehead to mine. Our breathing was strained, and I could feel my body clamped to his, holding him in place while our heart rates slowly returned to normal. "Wow, that was... I have no words," I spoke softly, not wanting to disturb this magical moment.

"I was jussst about to sssay the sssame thing," he spoke just as quietly, before I felt his body slip free of mine. He rolled off me and pulled me into his side. I tried to hide my yawn, but he noticed. "Did I finally wear you out?"

"Yes, but I don't know if I want to sleep just yet," I admitted into his chest.

"Sssleep, I'll be here when you wake. You need to ressst." He stroked my back while pulling the covers back up over us. I felt his lips press onto my forehead, as the warmth of his body and the steady sound of his heartbeat lulled me to sleep.

Maisie

The sound of voices hissing at each other woke me. I noticed that Emot wasn't in bed with me anymore, so I sat up. Keeping the sheet pressed to my chest, I noticed Sic and Kai standing off to the side of the room. They both looked pissed, as if they were arguing with Emot. He, on the other hand, looked relaxed and calm in the face of their anger. "It isss her decisssion and who caressss what order thingsss happen in. Ssshe is, at least officially, the Queen of the East Kingdom. When ssshe feelsss it isss right, I'm sssure she will consssummate yoursss asss well, but your petty fighting over the order is asssinine." Emot pushed away from the wall, and that was when he noticed me sitting up in bed.

He walked back to the bed and crawled towards me. "How did you ssssleep?" he asked, before pressing a kiss to my lips.

"Fairly well actually. What is going on?" I asked, as he scooted behind me, wrapping his arms around me.

"You sssmell like heaven. Like you and me combined," I blushed when he whispered in my ear, but then he spoke louder, "Thessse two sssseem to think they ssshould have been firssst, and they are mad at me." The others walked over, as I leaned back against Emot's chest.

"You said it was my choice, right? So, they shouldn't be mad at you, I chose." Both Kai and Sic had the grace to look chastised as they sat on the edge of the bed.

"You're right, it doesn't matter. The order is all your choice, and we need to remember that going forward." Sic's words were more to himself and Kai, as opposed to me or Emot.

"I'm well aware that it's her choice; I can still be fucking disappointed it wasn't me," Kai mumbled, feeling butthurt, no doubt.

I rolled my eyes as he pouted slightly, then Emot whispered in my ear. "He thinksss because you gave him a blowjob, he ssshould have been firssst." Emot's lips kept pressing kisses along my neck as he spoke.

"Would you stop that, it's distracting, and obviously, there is another reason they are here," I spoke, and Emot paused for a few moments to allow Sic a chance to speak.

"We need to plan on how to get Zugo back," Sic spoke diplomatically, rolling his eyes at Emot as he began to nuzzle my neck again. "Viper left a map of where we need to go, and the only safe way is by boat. What we need is someone who can make our ship invisible or disappear altogether. Maybe a trade ship would seem inconspicuous, if they still allow trade ships to dock in the North?"

"They do accept trade ships but only from Braceboro, the dragons there, trade with all of Lasina. Vago's laws have made all other trade nonexistent," Kai spoke up, making me wonder how he knew all the details. "I would have to contact Salzo to see if he is making a run there soon. He would let us on his ship and help us. Emot might have to fly to where he is docked."

Emot still had his nose buried where my shoulder and neck connected, but he mumbled, "I can do that, if we know where he issss docked."

"Who is Salzo?" I asked as I giggled, his scruffy chin tickling me.

"Salzo is a half dragon trader, he is much like Viper, only his mother was a dragon while his father was a sea krait. He has the ability to shift into a smaller dragon-like creature, but he can also breath underwater," Kai spoke, while Emot nipped my ear.

"Seriously, would you stop?" Pushing Emot's head away, he laughed. "How will we find him?" Emot slid to the edge of the bed and rose. I couldn't help but stare at his ass as he walked towards his room.

"Yaga might know where he is, or when his next shipment is arriving, and that will give us a hint of where he will be," Sic spoke, as he followed Emot's lead and headed towards his room. "Once we get ready, we will go find out," He said, as he closed the temporary curtain in his doorway.

Kai was already dressed in blue jeans and a tight shirt, so he just sat waiting, most likely to get a glimpse of my naked body when I stood. "So?" his question was followed by a raised eyebrow, and I blushed.

"So what?" I replied, pulling the sheet with me as I rose. Hopping off the bed, I felt a tug on the sheet. Kai was holding tight to the end and smiling a devilish smile. I huffed as I let the sheet go and marched into my closet. That was when I noticed the utter lack of mess between my thighs. it was going to take time to get used to that.

He followed me as I walked through the doors, closing them behind him. "Call me nosy but I want details of your first time with a basilisk." Kai leaned against the wood for a moment before stepping closer to me. He slid his hand down my ass and squeezed before burying his nose in my hair and breathing deeply. "You smell... satisfied, yet, like you could easily go for more."

I laughed at his assessment and stepped away from him. "Oh, come on, you know you wanna tell someone how it was," Kai teased, as I began to look for clothes.

"It was... wonderful I guess." I didn't know what else to say, so I left it at that.

"Wonderful? That's it, not mind blowing, not utterly disappointing, not I can't wait to sleep with Kai cause his cock is bigger and he knows how to work it just right?" Kai teased, making me laugh.

"Why is it always a competition to see who has the biggest dick? It isn't the size that matters, or in the case of basilisks, how many. It's all about how well you wield it," I tossed over my shoulder.

"And did he wield his well?" I felt him step up behind me and slid an arm around my waist. His fingers walking down towards the juncture of my thighs. "Did he make you cum, make you scream in pleasure?" His index finger swirled around my clit and I felt my head drop back onto his shoulder.

"Yes, he made me cum," I answered, and felt him pause his actions. The sound of disappointment I made caused him to resume his movements, swirling hard once more.

"I can't be happy that he pleasured you, but I shouldn't be resentful of you getting pleasure either." He slipped a finger

between my thighs deeper and pressed into my slit. "I want to be the one making you cry out as you cum." He added a second finger and I sighed as he began to move them.

"I really should get ready," I protested, but not really caring, as he continued to work my body.

"There was this one night." His thumb brushed my clit. "Where I was on watch, you must have been seventeen at the time." He stroked me faster. "I could smell your arousal, then I began to hear your soft pants. I couldn't help but stroke my own cock while you fingered yourself, wishing you were of age." His fingers curled and my body tightened around him. "The soft mewing sound you made when you orgasmed, had me cumming as well," his words tantalizingly erotic, and his fingers sent me over the edge.

He pressed his lips to my neck as I made that mewing sound just for him. "That's the sound I love hearing, it's almost better than when you scream in pleasure." He pulled his hand out from my legs and brought it up to his mouth, sucking his two fingers clean. I stepped out of his arms and turned as he finished sucking his fingers.

He smiled and stepped back towards the door. "I would love to lock this door and ravish you until you begged me to take you." I walked towards him, swaying my hips to entice him.

Pulling his head down, I kissed him. "But we have other places to be right now, so it will have to wait." I reached around him and opened the door while he captured my lips a second time. When he came up for air, I pushed him backwards out the closet door. "Now I'm going to get dressed and then we will put this rescue operation in motion, and hopefully save Zugo," with that, I slammed the door in Kai's shocked face.

Yaga's office was cozy, with lots of old books and his mate Ahxezo was a sweet old man who loved to bake. Ahxezo offered us tea and cookies while we waited for Yaga to look through his book to see when Salzo would return. "He was here about three months ago, so I would expect him not for another three. He only comes to the castle here once every six months." Yaga's voice boomed.

"So, we won't see him for twelve weeks still?" I asked crestfallen.

Yaga looked at me before practically yelling. "What?"

Ahxezo smiled as he handed me another cookie. "A month on Cazzith is the equivalent of two weeks on Earth. Our years are broken up into thirty-six months, while our days are only twenty hours. Our weeks are only four days long," he explained, as my mind cracked.

Emot laughed at the look on my face before speaking up. "The easiest way to explain is thusly, in Earth years I'm twenty-five, but in Cazzith years I'm actually thirty-eight. Sic is forty-four, while Kai is forty-one. You are technically twenty-seven, but since you lived on Earth and it was easier to go by Earth time for

the purposes of the Treaty, we did so." I could feel my mouth hanging open, but he continued, "There are five thousand seven hundred and sixty hours in a year on Cazzith, while Earth years are three thousand more hours than ours. So, six months is only forty-eight days. He was here twenty-four days ago."

"Ok, let me see if I got this, a day is twenty hours, a week is four days, a month is two weeks, and there are thirty-six months in a year." Sic nodded along with Ahxezo, and I rose. "I need some air." I walked outside into the red sunlight and stopped next to the wall. Kai caught up with me swiftly, making sure I was alright.

"I know it's hard to deal with, at first, but eventually, you will get used to our calendar and clocks," he spoke, as I looked up at him.

"It isn't that. When you were twenty-seven and I was eighteen, that's hard enough of a gap to deal with, now I find out, I'm actually twenty-seven and you're forty-one." My breathing began to increase while the yard around us blurred.

"Breathe, it isn't that bad, and if you prefer, we can continue to do this by Earth's time." He rubbed my back soothing me as I focused on my breathing.

"How are you okay with this? You're middle-aged and married to someone almost half your age." He had lived for forty-one years without a mate, and my heart broke for them all when I realized how long they had waited for me.

"I'm hardly middle-aged, Yaga is almost six hundred and fifty-three, that's four hundred twenty-nine in Earth years. I suspect Ahxezo is even older, but I would never ask." We began walking towards the main castle doors. "Why don't we get you

something to eat and then you can relax? Yaga probably knows where Salzo is and Emot can fly out to see if he will help us."

We were just about to walk into the castle when Sic stepped out of Yaga's door and called us over. We walked back towards Yaga's and reentered. Emot was sitting next to Yaga, looking over a map, as I stepped inside. He looked up and smiled at me while listening to Yaga talk about Salzo's normal route. Ahxezo was in the kitchen area cleaning up the dishes from tea, until Yaga finished his plate.

As he walked out of the kitchen, he paused just over the threshold and turned to look near the low fire. "I know you're there Yixe, you might as well show yourself." Without warning, Viper appeared on the floor slowly shifting into her human form.

"How do you always know?" she asked indignantly. "I thought you had outgrown your skills." He pulled her in for a fatherly hug just as Yaga looked up.

"Ah, Yixe my girl, how are you? How's Yoxe?" His smile was huge as he rose to pull her into a hug as well.

"We are both well, Grandfather." I stood staring with my mouth agape, as I learned that Viper was Yaga's granddaughter. "I came to help if I could. Who are you looking for?"

"Salzo. I just can't remember what his trade route is this time of year." Yaga's voice was loud in the pin dropping silence surrounding us. I looked at the guys and realized they were in similar state of shock as I was.

"Viper is your granddaughter?" I asked, and saw her blush, Viper actually blushed.

"Yes, she is our granddaughter. Our mate had her mother in our very last clutch. Her mother fell in love with a man from Wapeboia and they married. Yixe and Yoxe were twins. Yixe born in snake form, Yoxe in human, Yixe was wrapped around Yoxe when they were hatched from the same egg. It is very rare and magical that either was in human form," Ahxezo explained. "Many people call them shared souls. They have always remained together, as if needing the other to survive."

Viper looked at the map and then pointed to a small cove off the Northernmost point in the map. "This is the meeting point, and this," she moved her finger to another location, "is where Salzo is currently. If Emot leaves now Salzo can dock in the bay here and you can be there by the time he arrives." Viper hugged Ahxezo and Yaga one more time, and then waved. "I'll go help my sister get Zugo to the coast, we will be well hidden in the cliff caves," her last words said, she shifted into her snake form and disappeared.

Ahxezo and Yaga said goodbye as we all left their home and walked towards the castle. Kai and Sic led the way towards the kitchens as Emot and I trailed slowly behind. "Can I asssk one favor?" he whispered, pulling me to a stop halfway down the stairs. His body pressed me closer to the wall and he flicked his forked tongue along my neck. "If sssomething happensss to me, would you at least consssider having my child? It doesssn't have to be now, but sometime in the next five years."

His hand captured mine, threading our fingers together, before he brought it up to his lips and pressed a kiss to the back. "I know we haven't actually mated, but I want you to know how much I love you. I have for a long time, probably sssince an eight-year-old you asssked about the monsterssss. We all do, even if they won't admit it."

I felt my heart thump hard, it was too soon for declarations. I still didn't know if I wanted to stay here. He seemed to understand and pressed a kiss to my lips, his body rubbing along the front of me just right. "You don't have to sssay anything. I wanted to sssay the wordssss in cassse thisss went bad."

Kai popped his head back around the curve in the stairs and smirked, "Can I join?" Emot and I broke apart as Kai laughed, and Emot punched his shoulder.

"You're an assss," Emot said, as we began walking once more, his hand still wrapped around mine.

We entered the kitchen and Emot pressed one last kiss on my hand before he went to instruct the chefs. Kai poured me a small glass of some odd green colored drink and then raised his own. "You get one, and I would sip it slow, or you might float off."

Sic placed his hand over my glass and glared at Kai. "You can't give her that, she will be a wreck, and we can't have her drunk when we need to leave."

"Oh, come now Sic, I watered it down some, even mine." He winked at me as Sic rubbed his temples.

"What is it?" I asked, prompting Sic to throw his hands up in the air.

"I give up, you are a child, Kai." He pushed back and walked out of the kitchen, mumbling under his breath as he went.

"It's basilisk mead, and frankly, won't get you that drunk, he's more worried about the other side effects." His smile grew dangerous, and he downed his glass.

"And what might those side effects be?" I asked, as I lifted my glass to my nose and sniffed. The smell was earthy, and yet, there was a tinge of underlying sweetness, almost fruity, suggestive of a sweet flavor.

He grabbed my hand as I sat next to him and rubbed it along his cocks. I could feel how hard he was as he stroked himself with my hand. "It makes basilisks wanna fuck," he hissed into my hair, as his tongue flicked along my skin. "Gods you smell like sex, and it is so damn hot. I want my smell to be there with Emot's."

I laughed as I dragged my hand back to the table, and Emot placed three plates on the table. "Are you really that desssperate Kai?" he asked, as he picked up my cup and drained it.

I could almost see the ridges of his cocks twitching as he sat down. "Seriously, you just drank that. No, I wasn't desperate that's why I only gave her one." He pulled the bottle off the table and held it over the cup once more. "Want more?"

"No, I have to be able to fly in a few hoursss," Emot spoke, as he started eating his food. Kai filled his own cup and took a deep sip before sliding it towards me. I picked it up and took a small sip, just enough to taste it. The flavor was sweet, reminding me of a jolly rancher, and yet, there was a smooth heat that accompanied it.

Emot just shook his head and ate, as I took a larger sip before passing the cup back to Kai. "It's interesting, and I feel all warm and tingly." Kai's smile grew even larger as he dug into his own meal. Picking at the food on my plate, I was oddly aware of the tingling feeling between my thighs. I shifted in my seat to stop them, but the movement only made it worse. Squeezing my thighs together helped some, but only in turning me on more.

Kai and Emot finished their food swiftly and Emot picked up their plates, handing them to the girl cleaning the dishes. Kai looked at my plate and then me. "Are you done, or just not hungry?"

"I'm done. Thank you." Kai picked up my plate and rose, his cocks bulging in the front of his pants as he put it in the sink. Emot laughed at him as he walked back over to me, tilting his head slightly.

"You did, didn't you?" he said, reaching to take my hand. "Come on." I rose, only to realize my legs felt like Jell-O and my body was begging me to touch myself.

Emot picked me up and walked towards the door, as Kai ran to catch up. "Wait for me." I giggled as he sounded like a little kid to my ears. Emot didn't walk up the stairs to my room as I expected, but towards the garden instead.

"I can lock the door ssso he can't follow if you want or you can let him watch. If you really want, he can join?" Emot's words brushed my ear, as the guards opened the doors to the courtyard. He turned down a different path from the one Kai and I had taken the other night, Kai rushing to keep up.

Another door appeared and Emot opened it. "What'sss it gonna be?" he asked, while setting me down, the tingle between my thighs making me wetter just thinking about his cock. "Just fuck me please. I don't care." Kai snuck in and shut the door behind us, as Emot picked me up and placed me on a gardening table. He practically ripped my pants off while loosening his. I watched him stroke both his cocks as they knitted together and then he was sliding into me. Kai had his own massive cock in hand as he watched us.

"Fuck, thisss isss hot," he hissed, as he watched Emot fuck me hard and fast. Before I even realized what was happening, my body began to spasm around Emot's cock. I cried out in release as he kept working.

"I need more," Emot growled against my neck, pushing his pants off his hips. I watched as Kai stepped up behind Emot, then heard Emot's groan of pleasure. Emot continued to work my body harder as Kai pounded into his ass. The sight of Kai and Emot had my body racing towards another orgasm, and I screamed in pleasure as stars exploded in my vision. Emot roared as his cock pulsed deep and Kai groaned, pulling out to cum on Emot's back.

Collapsing back onto the table I felt Emot locked tight as a second moan sounded against my chest. I had completely forgotten that when they were combined, they got two orgasms. Kai's cock was still hard as he stroked himself fast, the erotic view was amazing, and he hissed as he came once more on Emot.

Once Emot slipped free, he helped me stand, pressing his lips to mine. "Better?" he asked, as we broke apart and Kai sat on the ground, looking up at us.

"I forgot how strong that shit was," Emot chuckled at Kai's words, and pulled his pants up. He helped me down off the table, before pulling his shirt off. He tossed the cum covered article at Kai, while I pulled my ruined pants back up as best I could.

"I have to go. Don't drink anymore of that while I'm gone, or you'll be ssstuck with one of them taking care of you," His words weren't mean, just letting me know that he was, at least, the devil I knew. I still wasn't sure I wanted to stay, and he was probably right. The less of them I slept with, the better off I was.

Kai buttoned his pants while standing and Emot kissed me one last time, before walking to the door. "I'll sssee you guyssss

tomorrow at the bay." He opened the door before shifting and flying up into the sky. I ran to the door to watch but he was already gone.

"He's too fast sometimes, but if you ask, maybe he will do tricks for you when we get back," Kai teased from beside me. "I'm sorry, I shouldn't have given you any mead."

"It's fine, I rather enjoyed watching you fuck Emot," my reply startled him so much, that he remained in the doorway even after I began walking towards the bedroom, my head held high.

Kai

I was still on fire by the time I walked into the bedroom, Maisie was in the shower and all I could think of was how much I wanted her body. "Having issues?" Sic's voice pulled me away from my thoughts.

"Just a little," I admitted, while he stood in his doorway.

"The whole castle heard her. Was it you or Emot?" he asked, his voice somewhat jealous.

"Emot," he looked shocked when I said this, and he smiled.

"Good for him." He turned to go back to his room when he called back over his shoulder, "You're welcome to come in if you want."

I walked after him, the curtain closing behind us. "I'm sorry about the other day. I was jealous, and I shouldn't have been. Emot made it perfectly clear that it has to be her choice, not ours, and he was right," Sic's words were soft, as he sat on his bed.

Sitting next to him, I flopped back onto his bed. "I get it, she has me tied in knots. We all want her, hell, we all love her, after years of watching over her how could we not? We just need to remember that all of us are allies, and who the real enemy is."

"Do you remember that time she was sitting in her window and she made a wish on the star?" Sic asked, making me smile.

"Yeah, she wished to meet the monsters under the bed," answering his question, as my mind played the memory again.

"I think that was about the time I realized fully that one day she would be ours, not just to protect but to love," Sic's words were quiet. "I think she was twelve at the time, and that was the first time Emot and I slept together. I don't know why the jealousy isn't there when I think about him with her, but it is with you."

"Probably because you love him just as much as her. Do you get jealous when I fuck him?" I asked, and felt him stiffen, giving me the answer without saying anything.

"Yes and no. Like, I can smell him on you right now, and it doesn't bother me, but some days, it bothers the hell out of me," Sic tried to explain.

"Well, at least you're being honest with me. The problem is that we have to share her. Frankly, once she lets me into her bed, I doubt I'll need you or Emot anymore, unless she asks for it." I heard her bathroom door open and looked toward the curtain. "Although, she did enjoy watching," I whispered.

He sat forward over me. "What? She was watching you fuck Emot?"

I looked back up at him. "Yes, and my guess is, she liked what she saw."

"Well, fuck." Sic sat back and we both heard the bedroom doors close. "We should go check on her."

"You go, I need to shower before I go around her again." I sat back up adjusting my cocks that were still hard, then stood. "Maybe next time, don't bite me so damn hard, that shit hurts, or maybe next time, I'll bite you," my last three words were suggestive, as I walked through the curtain and towards my own room.

Sitting by the fire, I let my hair drip dry while I slowly brushed it. I was thinking about the oddity that was the female basilisk when the door clicked behind me. Looking back over my shoulder I saw Sic walking around the couch. He smiled and sat on the cushions. "Want me to brush it?" he asked, as he held out his hand.

Placing the brush in his palm, I scooted back between his legs. He steadily ran it through my hair, as I watched the flames dance in front of me. "Why is the fire always lit? I mean I get that we enjoy the heat, but why is this one always lit?"

He paused for a moment, before continuing the rhythmic motions. "This was the first fire lit in the castle and will never go out as long as you remain here. Each basilisk nest has one fire that always remains lit. It's just a custom as old as we are, probably because it signifies prosperity, food, warmth, comfort, and home. It is sad when the nest flame goes out, it means someone has died, usually the female."

He braided my hair as we sat there. "Who tends them?" I asked, as he pulled more strands up into the braid.

"Well, here in the castle, we have several servants whose job it is to keep it going, in a normal home they will bank it at night. Some homes have gas flames like on Earth, others choose to add massive logs before bed and will get up throughout the night to check. It also depends on the size of the nest, and how many mates a female has." I pulled a ribbon out of his pocket and tied my hair to keep the braid in place as he paused.

"A female with four mates could expect that they would keep it going. If she only had one, then they would either have gas or bank it. When Thuzo and Sage mate they will live in a home here and have gas, but the first thing she will do once they marry is light that fire." He handed me the brush over my shoulder, and I noticed our reflection, he had perfectly French braided my hair.

"How did you learn to do that?" His eyes met mine in the mirror and he smiled softly.

"Your mother taught me, actually, when you were about nine. You were going through an only braided phase." He chuckled as if remembering me then.

"Why did you sign the Treaty knowing I was less than half your age?" My curiosity was running rampant tonight and, I guess, it has been on my mind.

"I am smack dab in the middle as far as my brothers are concerned. My mother has fourteen boys. My thought is, she was desperately trying for a girl, but that hasn't happened yet. She said she was done after my baby brother was born, he's five and a handful." He laughed and I giggled with him. "My mom may seem hard, but she wasn't always in agreement with this Treaty, she still only grudgingly accepts it. I think the main reason is because my older brothers were mated, and I was the one up next. Since then, the ones who could have mated, and there are only three unmated. One is about your age, one is six years younger and then the baby."

"Do you regret signing the Treaty?" I turned so that I was looking up at him, but he didn't look sad.

"Not at all. Yes, you were young, but it was an honor to bring Lasina lasting peace. I will admit, at first it was all duty, but once we began to get to know you, and we watched you grow, well, we all fell in love." He sheepishly rubbed his neck. "We all know it will take you time to get to know us, the way we know you. We also have to see what sort of changes bringing Zugo into this nest will bring. Who knows what he's been through?" I tried not to yawn while he was talking, but it didn't work.

"Come on." Sic rose and picked me up, carrying me back into the bedroom, before placing me on the large bed. "You should sleep, we have to leave at first light." He was about to go when I reached out and grabbed his hand.

"What, no goodnight kiss?" my words startled him for a moment, but then he gently pressed his lips to mine.

"Good night, Maisie," he whispered, as he covered me up once more, and then walked towards his own room.

"Good night, Sic." I yawned as sleep claimed me.

The red sun rose high over the castle as children ran around the courtyard. One little girl chased another, and several boys played with balls. Kai and Emot stood amidst the chaos, while Sic sat off to one side with a tiny girl in his lap, as they poured over a book together. I felt a set of hands slide around my stomach and a pair of lips touch my neck. "Come inside Mais, the

kids are fine, and you need to rest, before the Nymphs arrive tonight. Trust me, once they leave you will be up all night, dealing with the four of us."

The voice was soothing, as the arms pulled me back inside towards our bedroom. "Do you think they are happy?" I heard myself ask.

"They have you as a mother, four doting fathers and an entire Kingdom who loves them. There is so much love, it's hard to imagine them not being happy," the voice slid through me, as we arrived in the bedroom. His hand slid down my body and flicked the buttons of my pants open. "Let me make sure you feel loved too." His finger circled my clit before slowly rubbing my own wetness around.

I could feel the tension building in my core as he bent me forwards and slid the head of both his cocks along my slit. Working them both in slowly, then increasing as they rubbed my body right. My cries of pleasure increased as he began to shift them from two cocks to one, over and over. My back arched as I orgasmed around him, and I screamed out my pleasure.

I woke up as my body spasmed around nothing, the dream so lifelike it felt real. Something told me it was my basilisk fantasizing, and yet, I couldn't be sure if it was only her fantasy. My body ached from the dream, but I couldn't let myself break. I needed to keep myself away from the others. Kai walked out of his room and saw me sitting up in bed. "Is everything alright?"

Trying to calm my breathing, I replied, "I'm fine, it was just a dream."

His tongue flicked out swiftly and then he smiled. "Must have been one hell of a good dream." I felt myself blush as he

walked towards Sic's doorway and pulled the curtain back a bit. "Time to go, the carriage should be ready any moment."

I stood on the bed and walked to the edge only to have Kai stop me before I could get down. "We have a few minutes if you need me to take care of any lingering needs your dream might have aroused," his flirtatious words had me cocking an eyebrow at him.

"I'm perfectly capable of taking care of myself, thank you." His eyes darkened at the thought, and he pulled me off the bed to stand in front of him. He dipped his head and pressed his lips to mine for a moment.

When he pulled back, his eyes were hooded. "That may be true, but I can guarantee we could do better," he stepped back as he spoke, and let me walk towards my closet to get ready.

I dressed in comfy clothes and picked up the bag I had packed for the trip. Sic had said we would be gone for a week, or thereabouts, so I had thrown a few changes of clothes in my backpack. Once ready, I walked out the door into the bedroom. Sic was waiting for me and offered to carry my bag as we walked towards the outer doors. The castle was bustling like normal, as we walked down the stairs, and Thuzo waited by the main entrance.

"Your Majesties." He bowed before handing Sic a file. "These are the three men who were in the jailhouse when your captive was shot. Two have fled the castle grounds and there is currently a manhunt underway. I will notify you if anything changes upon your return."

"Thank you Thuzo," Sic replied, as he placed a hand on my lower back. "We shall, hopefully, be back in a few days. Make sure the castle remains secure and double the guards on patrol. If

you need to hire more men make sure they have been thoroughly vetted." Thuzo bowed once more and Sic escorted me out to the waiting carriage. The sun was just beginning to crest the horizon when I stepped inside.

30

Maisie

The carriage rolled on for hours as I watched the landscape pass. There were trees of all different colors and even the ones with bright purple leaves that hung down to the ground. Around lunch time, we stopped to let the unicorns rest and get water. Kai pulled a basket out of the back of the carriage and we walked into the shade that the trees provided.

He spread a blanket out so Sic could pull the food out of the basket. I walked around the clearing we were in and looked at the interesting plants surrounding us. One, in particular, captured my attention. It looked like a normal feathery fern plant, but it began to take on the shape of my face as I looked at it. Kai wrapped his hand around me as I looked over my shoulder. "Ahh, the Mimicking Laceflower. These little beauties will mimic any shape and typically will stay that way permanently."

Kai pulled me back to the blanket for lunch. Sic handed me a plate and I realized there were several different types of sandwiches and pastries on my plate. "Emot didn't know what type of lunch you would want so he had the kitchen make an assortment." I tried each one, eventually settling on the ham with a spicy honey spread and brie on it.

We ate in silence as the guards took their own break for lunch. I put my plate off to the side and rose. The plants around us captured my interest once more, as I noticed little emerald flowers blooming on a purple-leaf plant. "Those are Leatherleaf Mossapples. The fruit is emerald green as well. Also used in basilisk mead, for its enhancement properties, or aphrodisiac qualities," Kai's voice followed me across the clearing, and I felt a blush travel up my neck as I remembered the night before.

I turned back around and saw Sic walking back towards the carriage, rounding up the guards so we could continue on our journey. "I tell you what, I'll bring you back out here after we return. Just the two of us, and then we can play with the Laceflowers and eat apple blossoms," Kai spoke quietly, as he wrapped his arms around me. "We can make love as the sun sets."

He tipped my chin up and pressed a kiss to my lips before Sic's yell had us breaking apart. "Let's go, we still have a few hours to go."

Kai turned and held out his arm to walk me back to the carriage, the guards remounting their hellhounds as we approached. Once we climbed back up, I found myself pulled into Kai's lap, when we began moving again.

The sun began to set as the golden sea waters came into view, the red glow turning it a fiery orange, like a living flame on the water. A small seaside town sat at the mouth of the bay, small fishing boats dotted the water. Sic pointed out the lighthouse on the rocks as well as the large trading vessel just entering the port town. We followed the curved road into the town, stopping just as Emot stepped off the large ship onto the dock.

He strode up to the carriage as Sic opened the door and smiled. "Sssalzo sssaid he would help, and thanksss to Viper knowing hisss location, we can be there in a day or two." Emot pulled me out of the carriage and kissed me hard before Kai and Sic stepped down. "I missssed you," he whispered, as he broke our kiss.

"You've only been gone for a day," I said, as he pulled me close once more.

"That may be, but you forget we have been with you every night sssince you were eight." His breath caressed my neck as he pressed kisses up to my ear. "Maybe tonight we can let the sea do the work," my blush at his suggestive words traveled up my face, but I couldn't deny that I wanted him.

Sic was commanding the guards as a man jumped off the ship and began heading towards us. "Your Majesties." He bowed before me and the guys.

"Maisie, this is Salzo, Salzo, this is Her Majesty Queen Margaret," Emot introduced us, and I was taken aback by his unnatural beauty. Salzo had a dark black beard, with hints of silver running through it, framing his square jaw. His eyes were so light blue they looked silver in the fading light. I could see hints of tattoos covering his neck and arms, but they didn't look like normal tattoos, but more like scales. His crooked smile was warm and yet there was a twinkle in his eyes.

"It is nice to meet you, Salzo." I held out my hand to shake his, but he turned it and placed a kiss to the back.

"The pleasure is all mine. Viper has not stopped speaking of you since your return." He pulled me to his side and whispered into my ear, "You made quite an impression on my girl." I couldn't

help but laugh at his suggestive remark, as we began walking towards the ship.

Sic, Kai, and Emot walking closely behind us, to ensure nothing happened to me. Four of the twelve guards swept the ship to be safe before we climbed onboard, and Emot hopped back on to help me up. "Ignore Salzo's flirting, he flirts with anything that has a pulse."

"I heard that." Salzo laughed. "But you're not wrong."

This made Emot and I laugh as he scooped me up and carried me into the Captain's cabin. "Sssalzo sssaid you could have his room, while you are his guessst. We will ssstay on the lower deck with the crew." He set me down on my feet as Kai walked through the door with my bag.

"That is, unless you want us to stay in here with you," Kai winked at me as he spoke, making me smile.

"Go away, you big flirt." I shooed him out of the room and pulled Emot's mouth back to mine. "You, on the other hand, can stay." I kissed him hard, figuring the damage had been done the first time so I might as well enjoy the benefits of having him in my bed.

"Let'sss get you sssomething to eat, and then we will lock ourselves in here," his words caressed my lips, as we broke apart. A knock on the door announced Sic's arrival with a tray of food. He placed it on Salzo's desk before eyeing Emot and I.

"Salzo's about to cast off if you want to join us on deck. You will get to see the coast for a bit." He walked back towards the door and paused, "Unless you're tired of course, spending all day in a carriage can do that."

He closed the door as Emot watched him go. "What's hisss problem?"

"I don't fully know, but I think some of it is jealousy, maybe you should spend some time with him, instead of me." I pulled out of Emot's arms and walked to the tray. "I will stay here and eat, then maybe take a stroll on the deck."

"Maybe you would like two of usss in your bed tonight?" Emot's hands wrapped around my waist as I popped a piece of cheese into my mouth. "You ssseemed to enjoy watching Kai and I."

"We'll see, I do enjoy watching but, Sic is different, and I don't think just watching will satisfy him. I'm not ready for more," I admitted, and he kissed my neck before letting me go.

"I get it, and I'll talk to him." He walked to the door and opened it. "It will alwaysss be your choice," the door closed after he spoke, and I sank into the chair by the desk. That was the problem, I didn't know what I wanted anymore.

I picked at the food on the tray for a bit, suddenly not hungry. My mind kept going back and forth between leaving and staying. I still didn't know if my mother was alive, my heart still ached from what Sam had done, although not as much, since getting to know the guys a bit. The thoughts just continued to circle around and around. Pushing the tray around I stood, deciding I needed some air.

The evening was warm as we traveled further North, and the sky to the South was lit with a mermaid light show. I walked to the rear of the ship and watched the play of colors in the sky. A tiny moon hung low in the sky, but even being tiny it gave off a

large amount of light. Sic found me watching the lights in the sky and placed a hand over mine on the railing.

"It's a beautiful night, and the company even more so," I snorted a laugh at his words, and he frowned.

"I'm sorry, you flirting is like Kai trying to educate me on plant life. Somewhat ridiculous, and a bit out of character." He smiled but there was still something in his eyes that made me a bit uncomfortable. The look said he was only telling the truth, and he meant his words. I shivered before turning back to watch the sky.

"Are you cold? I can get you a blanket," he asked, pulling me closer.

"I'm fine really, I was just thinking about this rescue plan," I lied, just because I didn't want him prying into my thoughts.

"I think everything will be fine, we will rescue Zugo and then return to the castle without any problems." Sic wrapped his arms around me, his warmth seeping into my back. "What is worrying you about the plan?"

"I guess, just what happens after we rescue him," I whispered, hoping he wouldn't hear.

"You have all the control here. I will admit, I'm jealous of Kai when he is with you, and I will try to be better, but I'm not perfect," he spoke softly, his warm breath brushing over my hair. "Let's not worry about that now, what would you like to do tonight?"

I could feel the evidence of his desire pressing into my lower back and I slowly turned in his arms. Pulling him down for a kiss, I whispered right before our lips touched, "I want to watch

Kai fuck you." Opening my mouth to his probing tongue, he deepened our embrace before stepping back.

"As my Queen commands." His eyes were deadly serious but there was a tenderness in his voice that I couldn't place. He pulled my hand to his lips, pressing them to the back before walking off to find Kai.

31

Maisie

I walked back to the Captain's room and saw Emot standing in the doorway. He smiled as I approached, pulling me into his arms as soon as I was close enough. "Sssic sssaid you asked to watch them. Do you want me to sssstay as well or not?"

"I'm not quite ready to take that step with them, yet. So, maybe you... should stick around... that way I don't... go too far." He kissed me several times, halting my sentence several times. Pulling me into the room, he picked me up and carried me towards the bed. Laying me down slowly, he crawled onto the bed kissing me on any exposed area he could find.

"Do you want me to ssstop?" His lips hovered over mine and when I shook my head no, he dropped his lips to mine.

A knock sounded at the door, as he pulled back and smiled. "Time for the ssshow." I could feel the excitement rolling off him, and my own spiked up. Emot rolled so he wasn't blocking my view, curling himself behind me, as Sic and Kai walked into the room.

Kai shut the door and locked it before turning towards the bed, I could see the bulge in his pants signaling his own excitement. Sic stood facing the bed, his own pants pulled tight in

excitement. Emot lifted me onto my knees to face the two, while kneeling behind me. "Tell them what to do. Command them, for they are here for your pleasssure, just as I am," he kissed my neck, where it met my shoulder, as he spoke.

"I don't know what to say," I whispered back, while hiding my face towards his shoulder.

Emot slid his hand under my shirt and cupped the underside of my breast. "Tell Kai to take off Sssic's sssshirt." His thumb rubbed my nipple through my bra.

"Kai... take off Sic's shirt," I forced the words out, Emot's fingers, and my own nervousness, making it difficult.

Kai slowly stroked Sic's abs as he slid the shirt up slowly, mimicking the movements Emot made on my own body. Emot pulled my shirt off, and then unhooked my bra, Kai and Sic both watching his every move. "More, I wanna see more," I spoke up, a bit louder this time.

Kai began to unbutton Sic's pants, but I stopped him. "No." Emot took his own shirt off and tossed it to the floor.

"Tell him what you want, nothing isss forbidden here." Emot's warm chest pressed to my back and my head fell back onto his shoulder.

"I want Kai naked." The haze of desire began to overwhelm me as I watched Sic turn and begin to undress Kai. He slid Kai's shirt up and off, before unbuttoning his pants and slowly lowering to his knees, as he pulled them off. Kai's cocks were both hard and I wanted to watch Sic suck them both. As if he could read my mind, Sic licked first one head and then the other, while Emot worked his hand down the front of my pants.

The sight of Sic on his knees had my body growing wetter, aiding Emot's fingers as he circled my clit. He pressed two fingers into my pussy as Sic took one of Kai's cocks all the way to its base. Kai moaned and his head dropped back as Sic repeated his motions on the other side. "Do you want Kai to make Sssic sssuck one big cock or take both into his mouth together?" Emot whispered the question, as he used his free hand to push my pants down, giving him more access to my body.

"I don't know." I gasped as he began thrusting his hand. "I just want to watch them fuck, preferably, while you fuck me." Sic pulled both of Kai's cocks into his mouth and my jaw dropped open at his skill.

Emot kissed my shoulder, and then I felt cool scales brush my back as his basilisk rose to the surface. The silky feel turned me on more than I wanted to admit. He didn't shift fully, but let his scales rise to cover his skin. "Gods, my basssilisssk wantsss you sssso bad," his hiss more pronounced, as his forked tongue flicked my ear.

Pushing me forward onto all fours, he helped me pull my pants off as Sic stood and removed his. Kai pushed Sic towards the bed, as clothing was tossed over the side of it. Emot's naked body pressed along mine and I could feel his scales even on his chest. His arms wrapped around my waist and he lifted me clear off the mattress and placed me in his lap. I was still facing Sic and Kai, as Kai pushed him down onto the bed in front of me.

Once Sic was on his back Emot rose and slid closer, spreading my legs wide over Sic's face. "Bend forward," his words were a command, but still soft, and I bent forward, my face positioned almost to Sic's cocks, but I could see Kai's as well.

I felt a tongue flick out and circle my clit and looked down my body to see Sic spreading my folds as he licked me. Emot

pressed one of his cocks into my slit while Sic continued to lick me. "Oh fuck, yes," my words were moaned, as Emot slid fully in. I could tell from the difference that it was only one cock and not both together, but it still felt heavenly. His second cock pressed against my thigh as he began to move.

"Maisie," Kai spoke up, and I noticed him holding his massive cock by the base, both of Sic's were hard in anticipation as he rubbed the head against Sic's ass. I was mesmerized by the sight as he pressed in and then withdrew, inching himself into Sic. As he worked his cock into Sic, I felt a finger circle my own rear and tensed. I had never done anal and was somewhat scared, but Emot's finger only teased me. Kai eventually worked every inch of his dick into Sic, then paused, stroking Sic's cocks while I watched.

When he began to move, Sic groaned against my clit and I pressed back more, Emot's finger slipping into my ass. The shock had me holding still but it wasn't a bad sensation. "Sssorry sssweet, I wasn't going to go that far until you were ready," Emot's other hand caressed my back as he spoke.

As he tried to pull his finger out, sensation ran up my spine and I moaned. "More." I honestly didn't know what more I was asking for, I just needed more. He slid his finger back in and my pussy pulsed in excitement. "Yes." Kai continued to stroke Sic while sliding in and out, tempting me with the sight until I dipped my head and took one of Sic's cocks into my mouth. He groaned again and I felt Emot begin to press a second finger into my ass, the added stretch burning, and yet, feeling so amazing.

I continued to suck Sic's cock as I watched Kai fuck him, Emot working his own hips slowly behind me. "Do you want my other cock in your pussssssy?" Emot's hiss was thick, as he asked.

Releasing Sic with a popping sound, I looked back. "No." I couldn't voice the rest of what I wanted, my face blushing, even though I had three naked men with me.

Kai seemed to understand what I wasn't saying and said it for me. "I think she wants it in her ass." I groaned at his blunt words, but also in pleasure, as Emot moved his fingers just a bit faster.

"Isss that what you want Maisssie?" Emot asked, thrusting a bit faster with both his hips and his hand. I moaned my response and he chuckled.

Kai held up the cock I abandoned, and I slurped as I took Sic back into my mouth. Emot removed his fingers as he lifted his leg, hugging the side of my body. I felt him line the head of his second dick and press slowly back in with both. My body greedily opened for him and before I realized it, he was deep in both my ass and pussy. He held still until I began to wiggle, then started moving.

Sic's tongue still flicked my clit while also teasing Emot's cock. I could feel Kai's pounding as he rocked Sic, his moans of pleasure vibrating through my body, drawing mine tighter. Emot held onto my hips as he began to work faster. "That's its sugar, suck his cock good while we fuck you," Kai's words sent shivers of pleasure deep into my core, and I began to feel the tension build.

"Fuck, love, you feel ssso good," Emot whispered, as he began to move faster, pushing Sic's dick deeper into my mouth. I relaxed and took him all the way into the back of my throat. So, the fact that a snake can relax their entire throat was helpful in giving blow jobs, but I still didn't want to be one.

195

Sic moaned against my clit loudly, as his dick slid fully to the base into my mouth. The tension running through me snapped and I screamed around Sic's cock. My body clamping around both of Emot's cocks had him slamming hard, and he hissed loudly as he began to pulse inside me. Sic's cock jerked and I felt warm cum slide down my throat, while Kai held Sic's other cock away from my face.

Kai's other hand tightened in my hair as he slammed into Sic one final time. "Fuck, yesss," he said, as he pulled out to cum on the floor. I couldn't stop watching as jets of cum left the head of his cock, his hand stroking faster. He groaned a second time as he dropped to his knees, more cum escaping him.

Emot pulled me back so Sic's cock slid out of my throat. He sat back pulling out of me as Sic began to work his face out from between my legs. Once he was free, I collapsed onto the bed, my head hanging over the edge. Kai looked over at me and pressed a tender kiss to my lips. "Give daddy some sugar," his words made me laugh, as he kissed me the second time.

I felt Emot's body slide up mine before his head popped over the edge as well. "Did you really use that tired ass line? How about 'you' give daddy some sugar." He pulled Kai's face to his and planted a wet sloppy kiss on his lips, making me laugh even harder.

I rolled over just as Sic went to rise off the bed. "We should go so you can get some sleep." He pulled Kai up off the floor while grabbing his pants. Kai bent and cleaned the floor as he retrieved his own clothes.

Both began to walk out of the room as I spoke up. "You don't..." I bit my lower lip nervously. "You don't have to leave. You can sleep here." Kai turned and instantly began walking back

to the bed. Climbing in next to me, he pulled me close and kissed me again.

"You don't have to let us stay," Sic replied, as he turned to look at me, his hand still holding the doorknob.

"I know, but I would like it if you stayed," I spoke, as Kai trailed kisses across my face. "Would you stop that?" I pushed his head back and he grinned before pulling my hand to his lips.

"Cara mia." Kai began kissing up my arm as Sic walked back towards the bed. Emot tried to pull me away from Kai as I laughed at his antics, until Kai began kissing his arm as well, making me laugh even harder.

"Enough," I said, pulling my hand back and wiping the tears of laughter from my eyes. I tried to hide my yawn but failed as Emot pulled me closer, draping the covers over me. Sic blew out the lamp before climbing into the bed on the far side, behind Emot. Kai slid his arm around my waist sandwiching me between his chest and Emot's, the heat lulling me to sleep.

The room was chilled as I rolled over and grabbed the sheet. As soon as I got cozy once more, I began to hear whispers. "At least you got to mate with her," Kai's voice was almost too low to hear.

"Kai, it'sss not like that," Emot tried to calm Kai down.

"What fucking difference does that make? Mating is mating, and she is officially your Queen," Kai's words didn't exactly shock me, but I would disagree with his assessment.

197

"Fine, technically yesss, sssshe is my Queen, but we haven't mated," Emot spoke calmly, still in a hushed voice.

"Would you two stop arguing? As far as the Treaty goes, it's done," Sic's voice chimed in, and I tensed.

"What do you mean done? We weren't in any snake form."

"Sex is mating according to the Treaty we signed, it's binding. In other words, actual basilisk sex or not you are mated." My ears began to ring as Sic's words registered in my brain and my heart began to ache.

"That'sss why I sssaid it wassss her choice. It will alwaysss be her choice," Emot's voiced hissed a bit louder.

I felt my heart stop at Emot's words. He had known that even regular sex was bind us as mates according to the Treaty. The feeling of betrayal spread through me as they continued to talk. All I could hear was the blood rushing in my ears, as they kept talking.

Eventually I heard Sic hiss at the other two, "If you want to keep arguing about this let's take it outside." I closed my eyes, as they walked past silently, and waited for the door to close once more.

Once they were gone, I smothered a sob into the mattress, tears running slowly down my face. The thought that Emot had known hurt more than anything. I had known we would be legally bound, but not fully mated. Tears continued to fall, as I curled into myself. Pulling the sheets high over my head, I cried myself back to sleep.

I woke the next morning as the sun began to stream through the windows. Emot had returned to the bed at some point in the night, but the other two had gone to sleep elsewhere. He was wrapped around me, the big spoon to my little. I gingerly crawled out of the bed and pulled on a new set of clothes before heading up onto the deck, my thoughts still in turmoil.

Salzo was commanding his small crew while steering the boat closer to the large cliffs on our right. Walking to where Salzo was, I smiled at him as he focused on our course. "Good morning."

"Good morning, Your Majesty." He smiled back, then focused on the walls of the rock towering over us. "Did you sleep well?"

"Yes, thank you. I am sorry we inconvenienced you and thank you for your help in this rescue." He laughed and then looked over at me.

"You didn't inconvenience me, and when Viper says jump, I just can't help but jump. Cobra is the same way, those two have me wrapped around their little fingers, and they know it." He sighed as if he didn't mind their actions in the slightest.

"How long have you known Viper and Cobra?" I refrained from using their real names in case he didn't already know them.

"Actually, I grew up with Yixe and Yoxe. Our parents were friends. So, I'm seventy-two now, and they both just turned fifty this year." I still couldn't get my brain around the age thing here, and it must have shown on my face because he laughed. "I am forty-seven in human years, they are about thirty-three."

"I'm still getting used to the different time scale here. So, you knew them when they were children? What were they like?" His bark of laughter startled me, and he adjusted the large wheel heading directly for the cliff. My anxiety ratcheted up as he steered us straight for the wall and didn't turn away.

"They were just as much of a hand full then as they are now, but I love those girls. Don't tell them I said that, or I'll be eating my own balls for dinner." He laughed again at his joke, and I could visualize Viper feeding them to him with a spoon. While we spoke, the guys arrived on deck and I tried to ignore their presence, but my eyes kept traveling to them.

I gripped the rail in a white-knuckled grip to keep myself from going to them, their words still ringing in my ears. "Hold on, Your Majesty, this is going to feel weird," Salzo spoke, and I noticed we were about to hit the cliff wall. I almost screamed as the front of the boat hit the rocks, but it cut through instead of smashing.

"What the fuck?" I asked, as the ship began to disappear into the cliffside.

"It's a glamour to hide the entrance, I've been here so much I can see it without needing it to be removed. I spend quite a bit of time here when I'm not trading," Salzo explained, as I felt an odd tingle cross my skin. Once through, the dimly lit area was deep, but I could make out a dock further in. The massive cave swallowed the boat whole as if perfectly made for this purpose. We slowly pulled to the dock and then the crew jumped off and tied the boat up.

Emot walked up to me and pulled me close. "Do you want to ssstay here, or come with usss?"

I stepped back and looked up at him. His face was curious as he noticed my distance, but he didn't say anything about it. "I'll come with you."

He nodded as he walked back towards the others. I followed slowly with Salzo. "It shouldn't be dangerous, these caves are deep but hidden well. Viper and Cobra use them all the time, so they keep the riff raff out. Not to mention the glamour they keep up on this place," he trailed off as he stepped off the boat onto the dock. Emot held out his hand for me but I ignored it and kept walking, following Salzo as he led the way out.

32

Zugo

I collapsed onto the rough ground on the trail we were hiking, Viper and Cobra pausing to help me up. "I told you he needed a few more days," Cobra hissed at Viper.

"We didn't have that much time. Did you pack the cabin?" Viper asked in a hushed voice.

"Yes, all of it, including the fucking house," Cobra snapped back, holding up her wrist to show a bag. I had been amazed and a bit frightened, as Cobra had 'packed'. The entire house had shrunk down to the size of a teacup, then she picked it up and shoved it into a bag. We had left well before dawn and walked for hours, before camping that night. Upon waking, we started walking again and now as the sun hit its zenith, I was wiped out.

"We only have little ways to go and they should be here already." Viper held me up on one side while Cobra held up my other. I couldn't even think straight to talk, so I just let them carry my ass further up the trail. My eyes whipped up at the sound of a whistle and Viper sighed. "Thank the Gods."

Four men began to descend the trail rapidly. Within moments, we were surrounded, and two men took over for Viper and Cobra. They didn't even bother walking, just picked up my

legs and ran back towards the cliff. I expected to see a gap in the rocks but all I saw was more stone, until we were walking through what looked like earth. Viper and Cobra followed swiftly into the cool darkness as the men put me down. I collapsed onto the floor of the cave, enjoying the cool air that surrounded us.

Cobra placed a hand to my forehead and sighed. "We need to get him out of here, he's burning up. All my medical supplies are in the cabin." She shot a dirty look at her sister and I almost laughed.

"I have supplies on the ship," an older man spoke, while Viper twisted a finger in his beard. "Prince Kai do you think you can carry him back down to the ship?" A large hulking man stepped forward and scooped me up as if I weighed nothing.

"No problem," Kai, I assumed, said, as a beautiful blond walked into my view, with two other men. She was tiny compared to the men and yet she looked pissed. The erotic combination of restrained hostility wrapped into a tiny emerald green-eyed package had my cocks wanting to stir. Not that they could in my current state of exhaustion.

"Lord Zugo, allow me to introduce you to Her Majesty, Queen Margaret," Viper's voice took on a sensual quality, that had the man who was carrying me bristling, along with the taller of the two I could see. The third one, pulled Margaret closer as if staking his claim.

She pushed out of his arms and walked towards the older guy, Cobra and Viper. "You must be Cobra. I knew you were twins, just not identical ones." She shook Cobra's hand and I got a good look at her ass.

"We need to go, Your Majesty," Viper spoke up, and Kai began walking down a smooth path. Our little band moved

towards what looked like water, then I noticed the ship waiting there for us. For the first time in ten years, I could smell freedom, and I would not go back to captivity.

Queen Margaret walked up beside Kai and smiled at me. "You must be Zugo. It is a pleasure to meet you, however, I wish it had been under different circumstances." All I could do was gaze at her beauty and thank the Gods I had signed that damn Treaty.

Even without having to walk the last part of the path down to the ship, my vision began to blur. I tried to focus on Margaret's eyes, but they began to fade from my sight. I heard a muffled question, but didn't understand the words. She stopped the man and looked deep into my eyes, and the world went black.

Zugo passed out just as we were about to step onto the boat. I raced ahead of Kai and opened Salzo's door, so Kai could carry Zugo to the bed. Cobra rushed in behind us, demanding herbs and things, as she rushed to get water. Salzo opened a trunk that was pushed to one side and began pulling random things out before handing Cobra a large medical looking box.

"Your Majesty, if you would be so kind as to help me. The others can leave," Cobra's words brooked no argument, and Viper began to push the guys out of the room.

"Get this ship moving Salzo," Viper yelled, before slamming the door closed and locking it. She walked back to her sister, handing her a knife as she went. I watched as neither of them said a word, but began working in tandem to help Zugo.

"I knew it was too soon for him to travel so far." Cobra sliced through his pants and shirt. I went to sit at the head of the bed when Cobra's hand shot out and stopped me in my tracks. Zugo's body was covered with an odd-looking purple rash that reminded me of snakes crawling on his skin. "Fuck, he has Serpent Blight, get her out of here now," Cobra spoke to her sister, while nodding towards me.

"I'm sorry, Your Majesty, but you should go." Viper stood and began pulling me away from the bed. I tried to argue but she refused to let go of me as she pushed me towards the door. Opening it she pushed me out. I would have fallen if not for Emot's body catching me. "He has Serpent Blight and I highly doubt she's had it." She slammed the door once more and I heard the lock fall home.

I pushed out of Emot's arms and stormed past him and up onto the deck, just as we began to slice through the glamour once more. The sun was blinding after being in the cave for so long and I had to squint to see anything. Emot stepped up beside me and tried to pull me back into his arms. I couldn't help it, I pushed him away and yelled, "Don't!"

"Love, he will be fine, Ssserpent Blight is like human chicken pocksss, just really contagioussss," he spoke, thinking I was upset about Zugo.

"I'm not upset about him, you ass. I heard what you were talking about last night." I could feel the stupid tears gathering in my eyes. "You knew I wasn't ready to mate, and you did it anyway." I turned and began walking towards the front of the ship, needing some space.

"Maisssie, stop," Emot said, grabbing my hand, pulling me back to face him. "We didn't mate. Yes, we had sssex, yes, you knew that made you my Queen, but as far as our bassssilisssks go, we haven't mated." He pulled me into his arms. "I sssaid it was your choice and I meant it."

"Then why did they say we had mated?" I demanded to know, while trying to get out of his comforting embrace. I wanted to be mad, to make these stupid feelings go away, because I was slowly falling for them, and I couldn't let that happen.

"Becaussse they sssee ssssex as mating, in any form. The Treaty sssees sssex as mating, but that isn't what mating is. Mating is an emotional connection, sssomething that ssshould be taken more ssseriously than marriage, it'sss for life. A marriage can still be sssevered, a mating cannot," he explained loosening his grip slightly, as he tipped my chin up to look at him. "I would gladly mate with you Maisssie, but I know you aren't ready, and that's okay. It doesn't change how I feel, or the fact that you are my Queen. It only meansss we are legally wed according to the Treaty, but we haven't mated."

Seeing the sincerity in his eyes twisted my heart, but I couldn't fall, I just couldn't. I needed to get home, needed to make sure my mom was okay. This wasn't the life I wanted, I wanted normal. I stepped back out of his arms and whispered, "I just need some time alone." I felt my basilisk screaming for him as I walked away.

The sun was setting as I sat by the railing, our trip back was lit by the mermaid lights to the South. Viper found me all alone and joined me. "He will be fine. He woke up and his fever broke about twenty minutes ago. Cobra said you could go see him, but you can't get too close. She checked the others and they've all had Serpent Blight, so they won't get it again." She sat down on a box next to me sighing as she looked up to watch the sky. "So, why are you all alone?"

Huffing in frustration, I pinched the bridge of my nose. "They lied to me," stated simply, it didn't encompass enough of what I was feeling. "I don't know, Emot says we aren't mated, but Sic and Kai say we are, I just don't know who to believe, and then, also, I have to deal with Zugo. I'm just stressed," I let it all out, trusting that Viper wouldn't say anything.

"At any point during sex did you shift to full basilisk?" she asked, not beating around the bush.

"No, we were in human form the entire time," I admitted quietly, feeling a blush creep up. For Gods sake, I had fucked her and wasn't as embarrassed as I was talking about sex.

"Then you didn't mate." She laughed and I looked at her. "When Cobra and I came of age, our mom explained mating, and told us flat out that it would be impossible for us to actually 'Mate' unless we found other half-breeds. Basilisks mate in shifted form only, so if you didn't shift, you didn't mate," her explanation was simple and to the point, and I realized I needed to apologize to Emot. I had been a bitch to him for most of the day, and it wasn't fair.

I stood, gripping the railing tight. I still didn't know if I wanted to mate, hell, I didn't know if I wanted to stay here. "If you need time away, you can leave. You aren't bound here, and there is a huge world here to visit and explore," her words were beyond tempting, and I almost desperately wanted to do as she said.

"I couldn't travel the world, the Treaty says we only have a year to consummate the marriages, or a war breaks out," I said sadly, not bothering to tell her that I wouldn't be here for much longer.

She stepped up to the rail next to me and hugged me. "Be safe, the world is not what it seems, nor are the people," her cryptic words had me turning, but she was already walking away. "Oh, your men, for the record, are all wonderful men, not like your father," she tossed over her shoulder, then kept walking.

The feeling that she knew what I planned to do unsettled me, but I didn't think she would tell the guys. I stood watching the

lights in the sky for a few more minutes and then turned to go check on Zugo. Hopefully, he would recover quickly, and at least one good thing would come out of my time here. We had rescued him, so he could live his own life now.

I took a deep breath before turning away from the railing. The guys were all by Salzo, and I could feel their eyes tracking me as I moved. They had given me space, but they were always hovering. Walking down below, I knocked on the door to the Captain's room. Cobra opened it with a smile and gestured for me to come in. Zugo was propped up on pillows with a cup of something in his hand, the steam rising towards his face.

"It's good to see you awake," I commented, unsure of what else to say, the awkwardness of meeting someone new as they lay naked in bed, sick.

"I am so sorry, Your Majesty, it seems I have taken your room," Zugo's voice was smooth, and flowed over my skin like silk. If I had decided to stay, I could tell he would be trouble for me.

"It's no trouble really, I can find somewhere else if I get tired." Cobra set a chair beside the bed for me and I sat next to her.

"He is doing much better, Your Majesty," Cobra spoke softly, as she tipped his cup, making him drink. "He shouldn't be contagious after tomorrow, and the rash will go away in about a week."

"Please, both of you, stop calling me Your Majesty. My name is Maisie, and I would prefer to be called that," I said, but smiled at Cobra indicating I had heard her.

"It is hard to call you anything but your title, Your Maj..." she stopped, when I glared at her, "Maisie. We both grew up in the North, and your father was very demanding of what he felt was his rightful form of address. He once had a man beheaded for saying 'Your Highness' and not 'Your Majesty'." She shuddered as if she had been there and seen it.

"Cobra, can you give me a hand?" Viper's head popped around the corner of the door, as she spoke.

"Sure." She patted my knee, and then smiled at Zugo. "You drink all of that tonic, and you make sure he does," she spoke to both of us in turn and then rose, following her sister out the door.

The silence that descended was charged with something, but I couldn't quite put my finger on it. He stared at me with beautiful blue eyes, and his chiseled jaw was covered in scruff. I twisted my hands in my lap trying to find something to say when I realized I was staring at his chest. He was leaner than the others, but I could tell with a few good meals and some weight he would fill out and be just as defined as they were.

My eyes almost trailed farther towards his lap when he spoke up, "Thank you, for saving me, or sending Viper to save me. I don't know how to repay you, but I will spend the rest of our lives making it up to you."

"I'm sorry you were jailed just because you signed a piece of paper." I realized that all this was my fault. For being born a girl, for my mother marrying me off, for him being trapped all these years. Swiftly rising I walked to the door before the tears in my eyes could fall. When my hand hit the doorknob, I heard his voice, "Please don't leave."

Dropping the knob, I tried to wipe my eyes before I turned around. "I'm sorry, this is all my fault," I said, returning to my vacated chair.

"It's not your fault. You aren't responsible for me signing the Treaty, you aren't responsible for your father's actions. He's nuts if I'm being honest, and from the rumors, you might not be his." My eyes snapped up at that and he smiled. "I'm only teasing, he started that rumor just after your mother left, but you have his eyes."

I shuddered at his assessment of having any visible likeness to the man that tried to kill my mother and me. "Did you know him well?" I asked, curious about him, but also judging how much I could trust him.

"I didn't really know him at all. Most of the aristocracy are required to attend court several times a year. I was still young when my parents died, and after signing the Treaty, he threw me in jail." His eyes seemed to drift off as if he were remembering his time locked up and I rubbed my arm nervously.

"How old were you when you signed the Treaty. You said you were young, so how young?" I had the sinking suspicion I wasn't going to like his answer.

"I was about thirteen, almost fourteen. My uncle was the one who suggested I sign it, then after I signed it, he told the king. No doubt trying to take my title, unfortunately for him, the King killed him and locked me up." I felt my jaw drop when he said thirteen, he was barely older than me.

"Wait, basilisk years or human years?" If he was speaking in human years then he was barely younger than Emot, but basilisk years were different.

"Cazzith years, not Earth years," his words sent my mind into a frenzy, that meant he was younger in human years but how much younger.

I tried to do the math in my head and realized I had no idea how to do that. I started counting on my fingers, feeling my face scrunch in concentration. "God, I wish I had a calculator right now. Hell, I wish I knew the conversion rate better, I suck at math. I was always a history nerd, why didn't I pay more attention in algebra?"

"I was nine in human years," his words interrupted my ramblings.

"Nine? You were nine when you signed the Treaty? Why? Who would let a child sign a legal document like that? Did no one give you proper legal representation?" Besides the stupidity of allowing a child to sign anything so binding, I began to realize my father had thrown him in a dungeon not long after signing. I stood up and began to pace the room mumbling to myself as I walked.

"My father threw a nine-year-old into a dungeon?" I looked at Zugo. "Alone?" His nod made me ramble again, "That was a stupid question of course alone, who or what else would he have locked in there? A litter of puppies and kittens? There is something really fucked up with that man. How can I be related to that kind of monster? I just don't get it!" My mind whirled as I continued my diatribe against my father.

"You know, you're kind of beautiful when you get all indignant," Zugo's words didn't register at first, but I turned and looked at him knowing he had said something.

"What did you say?" I asked, and I saw him blush bright red.

"I said you're beautiful," he smiled as he said it, causing me to blush along with him.

"I'm sorry for ranting, I just don't understand how they could have let you sign something like that so young." I walked back to the chair and sat down once more, trying to calm my anger.

"I did it for the good of all Lasina. The wars and fighting were bad, but your father is even worse. He wants all of this country for himself, and I wouldn't be surprised if he tries to kill for it." He coughed a bit and I rose to hand him his cup, our fingers brushing. I felt a tingle slide up my spine and my basilisk hissed 'Mine' in my head. "Thank you."

"Are you feeling any better?" I asked, while he took a drink.

"I feel a bit better, but I still feel weak. The downside of being a snake is that we don't require food but once a week. So, I

was only fed once a week." I could feel the tears building behind my eyes but tried to keep them at bay.

"Please don't cry, it wasn't my intention to upset you." Zugo leaned over to the side of the bed and wiped a tear from my face. "Even when you cry, you're beautiful."

I sniffed and laughed, wiping my face on my sleeve. "I just feel guilty that practically your whole life was spent in a dungeon. I mean, no games with friends, no first date... Ohhhh... Are you a virgin?" I snapped my lips shut, as the question rolled out of my mouth, and instantly went red. "Never mind don't answer that."

His rich laughter filled the room for a moment. "I knew I liked you from the moment I saw you. Yes, is the answer, not that it matters. You are right, I haven't had a first date, or first kiss, or first anything really. I'm okay with you getting those firsts, if you are." I couldn't help but smile, he was so sweet, despite being locked up for so long. How was he not broken, damaged beyond all repair?

He yawned behind his hand, then handed me the cup he still held. "You should get some sleep. I look forward to getting to know you more." The strange thing was, I wasn't lying when I said it. I still planned on leaving, but oddly I did want to get to know him more. In fact, I kinda wanted to get to know all of them more. I rose from the chair and placed his cup off to the side. "Sleep well, I'll see you in the morning."

"Sweet dreams, beautiful." He spoke as I opened the door and I couldn't help but smile and shake my head at his flirting. I stepped out into the darkness and closed the door behind me.

I walked around the deck for a bit, the sky still a dark purple, the lights had stopped to the South and I missed their beautiful glow. Emot found me standing by the railing watching

the waves. The occasional tentacle breached the water in the moonlight as I looked towards the unknown. "You ssshould try to sssleep, love," he spoke softly, as he stepped up next to me.

"I know, I just can't help but think this is all my fault. You all lost your freedom and a lifetime of experiences just for peace." Emot pulled me close and hugged me, as we stood by the railing.

"Maisssie, we didn't lossse out on anything. Basssilisssks live a long time, and we have plenty of yearsss ahead of usss to make up for that time." He turned me in his arms and tipped my chin up. "It'sss one of the reasonsss we sssaid it's your choice, for everything, sex, mating, kidsss... it will alwaysss be your choice." He lowered his head slowly allowing me to back off if I chose to, but I didn't. His lips pressed against mine in a tender kiss, his arms pulling me closer to his chest. When we broke apart, he smiled. "Let's get you to a bed, you look like you're about to fall asleep standing up."

Salzo woke the guys as we neared the town, which I learned was called Mistshore. We slowly docked and the crew tied the ship up securely. Viper and Cobra were talking to Salzo as I watched the men work, he laughed at something they said and then kissed both their hands. Viper walked up to me and stood by the railing. "Dry land once more."

"I enjoyed sailing, this was my first time, but I liked it." Viper laughed at my assessment.

"You won't if you're ever in a storm." Cobra joined us sighing as she looked at Mistshore.

"Where are we going now, sister? We have no place to put our cabin down." Cobra held up her bag and shook it accusingly at Viper.

"Well, we have plenty of room at the castle, and I'm sure the guys would know a place nearby for your home, if you don't want to stay in the palace," I offered, not regretting it a bit. I liked Viper and Cobra, they seemed to be similar, so I didn't foresee any issues.

"That would be lovely, Your... Maisie," Cobra replied, and Viper laughed.

"Oh, don't sound so hoity toity, she's not like the other Queens we've had to deal with in our lives," Vipers words piqued my curiosity, and I fully intended to ask her about it if I ever came back. I still knew I needed to get moving and make sure my mother was alright.

I watched the ship's crew drop the gangplank for us to disembark, as Kai helped Zugo out of Salzo's room. Cobra rushed over to check on the patient but deemed him well enough to walk to the inn near the docks so Emot helped him stand as Kai and Sic walked off the boat heading for the inn.

I stepped off the boat onto the dock just behind the guys. Cobra had deemed Zugo still too weak to travel long distances, so our rescue mission was stalled in Mistshore. Kai and Sic went to book rooms while Emot helped Zugo walk slowly off the boat. I still wasn't allowed to touch him, but I didn't plan to be anywhere near any of them by midday. Cobra and Viper walked down the dock towards me smiling. "Thank you for letting us come to the castle," Viper spoke, as she hugged me tight. "Be safe."

I felt her press something cold into my hand and when she stepped back, she winked. Looking at my hand, I found a dagger in my tight grip. "What is this for?" I asked, but they were already out of earshot. Slipping the dagger into my bag I began to follow the guys, but not so close that I couldn't slip away. I was going to find a way home.

I paused as Emot and Zugo entered the inn that Kai and Sic had gone into, then turned and walked the other way. "Your Majesty." Fuck, I forgot about the guards. "Shouldn't you be going to rest?" the man asked, standing just in front of me.

"Am I not allowed to walk around? I'm not tired and I would like to explore the town a bit while they get settled." I

pulled my most royal attitude about me, not that I had much of one.

"I'll get a guard to go with you," he spoke, while waving over one of the other guards. The woman had brown hair, brown eyes, and I swear, brown everything. "This is Ajih, she is one of my finest. Enjoy your walk, Your Majesty." I smiled at Ajih then turned rolling my eyes as I started walking again.

She followed me closely, until we reached an area that had several stalls with venders. I slowed, looking at items here and there, hoping she would get bored. More vendors were beginning to arrive as the sun rose higher. Peeking over my shoulder, I noticed Ajih keeping up, but every once in a while, she would look away. If I timed it right, I could slip away.

I slowly walked to the next stall, when a familiar face caught my attention, but when I looked fully it was gone. The lady selling jewelry smiled as I approached her, picking up a beautiful emerald necklace. "It matches Your Majesty's eyes. The finest Asitrine this side of the Falto Sea. Please take it as a gift."

"I couldn't really," I said, but she pressed the necklace into my hand and wouldn't take it back.

"It is a gift, for protection." She went to help another customer, so I shrugged and put it in my pocket. Ajih turned towards a nut vender for a moment as I began to walk again. She turned back too quickly for me to make my escape, but as I glanced back at her, I could've sworn I saw my ex, Sam.

I shook off the ridiculous idea and kept walking. Another vender waved me over, her display covered in all sorts of Earthly items. "Would Your Majesty like something to remind her of Earth?" Looking over her table I felt a chill crawl up my spine as if someone was watching me but shook it off since I knew Ajih was

watching me. I picked up the digital camera, making the woman smile. "Does Your Majesty like the camera?" I nodded my head as she smiled. "Then take it, it's yours."

I pulled my backpack out, unzipping the large pocket and sliding the camera in for safe keeping. Just as I stood up, I felt someone run past me, knocking me off balance. Ajih took off after the younger boy. The market was in chaos as the young boy zigzagged away, I felt a hand slide into mine, then I was being pulled into an alley between two buildings.

I was about to scream out when a hand slipped over my mouth. "Shhh, it's me." Sam's face entered my vision causing me to jerk back.

"What are you doing here? How did you even get to Lasina?" The shock of seeing him outweighing the fact that he had cheated on me.

"Your father kidnapped me, and brought me here, I was able to get away from him, and I came looking for you." Sam looked around before pulling me further away from the market.

"I found a woman who will help get us back to Earth. Then we can run away like we planned," Sam spoke swiftly, as he pulled me through empty streets towards the edge of the town.

I dug my heels in and he stopped for a second. "Did you forget that I caught you with Pamela Conrad, the night before we were supposed to elope?" I shook his hand off and crossed my arms over my chest.

"I know, and it was stupid of me, she just wouldn't take no for an answer. I followed you, and went to your house, which is where I met your dad." He pulled me closer to him intending to kiss me, but I turned my face, so he hit my cheek instead. "I'm

221

sorry, Maisie, really I am. I just want to go home, and we can forget all of this. Start fresh just the two of us. Please, I love you."

Realizing a small part of me still wanted his words to be true, I nodded. "Let's go then. Where is this woman you spoke of?" He smiled, as he began leading the way to the edge of the town once more.

"She has a house just outside of town, in the forest. If we hurry, we can be home by lunch time. Your mom will be so happy to see you." My heart kicked up a notch as he spoke of my mom, hope filling me that she was still alive.

"Was she alright when you were taken?" I needed any information I could get about her. The last I had seen was Vago throwing my mom across my bedroom and slammed her to the wall.

"She was unconscious, but she looked fine when I arrived, then your dad grabbed me and left." We stopped at the edge of the town and Sam looked both ways before pulling me to the forest's edge. Once we were inside the cover of the trees he slowed. "Good, now we don't need to run anymore."

"Do you know where we are going?" I asked, as he picked his way over a log then helped me over.

"There is a clearing a few miles from here that we are supposed to meet at, the lady said she would make a portal for us," he spoke, as he kept heading North. "It shouldn't take but a few hours to get there." I looked back over my shoulder, back towards where Kai, Sic, Emot, and Zugo were, wondering if they knew I was gone yet, and oddly missing them.

The sun was high overhead by the time we exited the woods. A large open clearing spread out before us, devoid of any life. "I thought you said she would be here." I looked at Sam as he continued to pull me forward. All I wanted was to sit for a few minutes, but he hadn't relented about needing to keep going.

"She should be here any moment," his words sounded different, like he was hiding something from me. When I turned to ask him what was going on, he threw me to the ground hard. "You know, it was so easy to get you away from there. You are so gullible and naive."

"What are you talking about? I thought you said you loved me." I tried to stand but he kicked me back down to the grass. Dropping to his knees in front of me.

"Stay down if you know what's good for you." He stood just as I began to hear the sound of marching coming from behind me. An army of guards marched towards us from the North. Sam waved a hand as they came up running to surround us. "I did my job now, let me go home," he spoke to someone I couldn't see.

"Sam why are you doing this? I thought you loved me." His twisted smile was all I could see as he knelt in front of me.

He captured my chin in his hand and forced me to look up at him fully. The hatred on his face was as clear as day. "As if I would ever love a monster like you." He pushed me back onto my back and a shadow covered my face.

The sunlight haloed the large figure as he bent lower. "Hello, Margaret, my darling daughter." Vago's eyes shone bright green just before he punched me in the face and knocked me out.

223

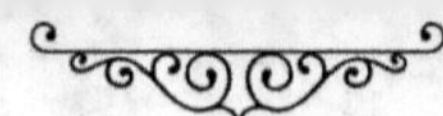

Vago

"Pick the bitch up and kill the kid." I didn't bother making sure my commands were followed. I just walked back towards where the guards had hidden my carriage. The fact that I had needed to travel all the way here, just for the bitch of my daughter, pissed me off.

"Your Majesty, please just send me home, I won't tell a soul, I swear," the kid blubbered, and then I heard the sound of a sword exiting its sheath. "Please." They always begged, and most days I loved the sound of begging, but hearing him beg just made me want to torture him.

"Wait." The blade stopped inches from the kid's neck. "Bring him back with us, so I can watch him die slowly." A guard was carrying Margaret's limp form, ogling her tits as she hung across his arms. He would die for that, but I wasn't about to carry her myself so it would have to wait. I turned as the sounds of a scuffle reached me and watched as the kid tried to fight off the guards holding him.

"If you can't behave, I'll just have them kill you and leave your body to rot in this clearing." He continued to fight, so I stopped, pulled my dagger from my belt and walked back to him. I

didn't bother waiting for his blubbering to stop just shoved the blade into his heart and then let go. "Leave him."

The guards dropped his body as he began to bleed out, and I wiped my hand on my handkerchief, before tossing it to the ground. Margaret was beginning to come around as I began walking once more. I needed to get her back to the Northern territory before the Princes realized she was missing. Then, I could take over all of Lasina, and rule as I always should have.

Margaret fought as she woke up and I barked at the guard carrying her. "Just knock her back out." He bellowed in pain as she bit him, making him drop her to the ground. She stood up on wobbly legs and tried to run. She got as far as Sam's body before noticing it and screaming. Another guard caught up with her and hit her on the back of the head catching her before she could fall. I pointed to the guard who had dropped her. "Kill him." Another guard ran him through, while the one carrying Margaret followed me into the tree line.

The carriage door opened as the footman saw us coming and I stepped inside. "Put her here," I told the guard holding Margaret. While placing her on the seat a necklace dropped to the ground. He went to get it when I spoke, "Leave it, get moving." The door slammed, leaving me in cool darkness, then the carriage lurched forward.

I couldn't help but stare at the prone body lying on the carriage seat across from me. She looked so much like Clara that my mind went back to our wedding day. Clara's blond curls had been piled high, her cream-colored dress fit her slender frame perfectly, and the way the sun had tinted her skin had made my mouth water. Margaret looked just like Clara had on our wedding day, only younger. We had been so in love, even planning on taking over all of Lasina together. It was only after she got pregnant with Margaret that she had decided she wanted no part

in it. We had fought often after that, and eventually, she had fled. But I had found her, and now she was where she belonged.

Acknowledgements

Thank you to all my wonderful readers, I hope you enjoyed the first book of The Lasina Chronicles series.

Thank you to my wonderful Alpha readers, Teresa, Everly, Melody, Ira, and Cassy. This series has been a wild ride and I am grateful to you all for hanging on with both hands.

Mindy G and Krystal, I am truly grateful to have you both in my life; and I hope this series becomes a cherished one, snakes and

About the Author

Rozie Marshall is an inspired writer from Colorado, where she lives with her husband, kids, and fur babies. She has a BA in European History and works in a bookstore, where else? Although she started writing over a decade and a half ago, it took some convincing for her to publish her first book, but once it happened, the floodgates of words burst, and the books kept coming.

Often referred to by her fans as Goddess of Smut and All That is Sexy, she delights her fans with her special knack for kink and smut. When she is not busy arguing with her characters, she spends her time plotting new stories and doing research for her books. Oh, and coffee is her best friend.

You can find out more about Rozie Marshall and follow her updates by joining her Facebook Group and subscribing to her Newsletter.

Website: https://www.roziemarshall.com/

Facebook: https://www.facebook.com/RozieMashall/

Facebook Group:
https://www.facebook.com/groups/RozieMarshallBooks/

Follow me on Amazon: https://www.amazon.com/author/roziemarshall

Claimed by the Goddess Series

Triad Found – Available on Kindle Unlimited

Pentacle Bound – Available on Kindle Unlimited

Elements Tamed – Available on Kindle Unlimited

Goddess Claimed – Available on Kindle Unlimited

Magic Unleashed – Available on Kindle Unlimited

Eight Deadly Sins

Lilith's story will continue in Original Sin

Original Sin – Coming Soon

Love Bites

Bite of My Life Prequel – Available on Kindle Unlimited

Sisters of the Seven Seas

Silver Sails – Available on Kindle Unlimited

The Lasina Chronicles

The Basilisk Princess – Available Wide

The Basilisk Queen – Available Wide

The Basilisk Empress – Available Wide

Personal Harem Series

Red's Rangers – Available on Kindle Unlimited

Fallen Petals – Available on Kindle Unlimited

Brothel of the Damned

Cowritten with Clover Payne, C.T. Dracass, & Melody Calder

Deadly Desires – Available on Kindle Unlimited

Deadly Liaison – Available on Kindly Unlimited

Anthologies

Anonymous: A BDSM Anthology

Anonymous Part 2: A BDSM Anthology

The Devil's Playground

Stand Alone

Twisted & Torn: A Dragon's Tail – Available on Kindle

A Thief's Lover – Available on Kindle